The Garden of Good Things

A.M. Offenwanger

amovitam press

amovitam press

100% Human-Made – No generative AI was used to create the content or cover of this book.

Note: This book uses Canadian spelling and punctuation.

Also by A.M. Offenwanger

THE SEPTIMUS SERIES

Seventh Son

Cat and Mouse

Lavender's Blue (A Septimus Short Story)

Checkmate

Star Bright

Standalone:

Martin Millerson: A Retelling of "Puss in Boots"

Novellas:

The Twelve Days of Christmas: A Tale of Christmastide. With Elves.

The Forty-Dollar Christmas: A Canadian Holiday Story

Contents

The Letter

"Once upon a time," Nina's grandmother told her, "there was a garden. It was full of good things to eat—carrots and pumpkins and tomatoes and strawberries and lettuces and apples and peas—and of beautiful flowers, some of which were good to eat too. One day, a little girl walked into the garden..."

Nina smiled at the memory of Granny's dreamy voice, so soft, a little bit scratchy from all the Marlboroughs she'd smoked over the years. Granny was gone now, had been for more than a decade. There wasn't much Nina had left of her, only a blue glass paper weight she kept on her desk, and her memories. Granny had spent her last few years in an old folks' home, her little house sold to pay for the fees. In the end she hadn't even recognized Nina anymore.

Nina looked down at the letter in her hands.

"Dear Ms. Takahashi," it read, *"it is our pleasure to inform you that you are the sole beneficiary and legatee under*

the will of the late Miranda McManus of Hawthorn Lane, Houghton, B.C. The property in question includes a cottage with adjacent garden. Please contact our office for particulars at your earliest convenience. Sincerely, James Spreckles; Spreckles, Masters and Miffling, Attorneys at Law."

A garden. That's what had brought back that memory of Granny's story of the Garden of Good Things. A garden that was entirely fictional, that came from a fairy tale...

Nina shook herself and came back to her surroundings. She stared out the window at the bleak cement wall of the law offices across the alleyway, where a slow dribble of water left a dark streak down the dreary grey surface. The rain had been incessant in the last week, not letting up even once. Typical Vancouver weather—for winter. This was summer; it was supposed to be sunny and nice, but it felt like November out there.

Nina's hand tightened on the letter. This had to be a mistake, probably a variant of one of those millionaire scams. "Contact us, and you'll come into a lot of money." Sure, and if you buy that, I've got a bridge to sell you too. Who on earth was Miranda McManus? Nina had never heard of this person before.

She balled up the paper and slam-dunked it into the wastepaper basket. Forget beautiful gardens full of good things; they didn't exist. What existed were rain-soaked city streets where cars hissed by in an endless stream of metal and fumes, and stacks of files—well, electronic stacks, anyway—that needed to be dealt with or Nina's boss June would throw a fit. Never mind that Nina had come in in her time off to deal with it all.

But then, if she hadn't, she wouldn't have found this letter... Nina retrieved the letter from the garbage and smoothed it out. "Please contact our office at your earliest convenience..." Well, it wasn't convenient. Was it? Nobody would be there, in an attorneys' office, at this time of day anyway.

Nina stared at the phone number on the letterhead, and then at her phone, which, somehow, was in her other hand. Nobody would be there, and it wasn't convenient. And who was Miranda McManus, anyway?

As if they were acting of their own volition, her fingers typed out the attorney's number.

Google Maps

The voice navigator of Google Maps squawked at Nina from her phone on the dashboard. "In two. Hundred. Metres. Your destination. Will be. On the right!" it insisted in its eternally-cheerful-yet-hectoring tones. Nina had been driving through dense pine forests for at least an hour, although up until the last turn it had been all paved roads. She slowed down her car, but there wasn't anything on the right, just a tall, ragged hedge among the trees, overgrown and weedy-looking. Certainly no house. She slowly let the car roll past the long line of unkempt bushes, crunching over the gravel of the road. "Take. A left turn, then. Make. A U-turn," the voice navigator instructed.

"Oh, shut up," Nina muttered and kept going.

"Take. A left turn, then. Make. A U-turn," it repeated.

"But there's nothing there! Only a silly hedge," Nina told it.

"Make. A U-turn. Then continue. For one. Hundred. Metres. Your destination. Will be. On the left."

"Fine!" Nina shouted in exasperation and cranked the steering wheel, swinging the car around in the narrow country lane. She nearly got stuck in the ditch on the opposite side of the road. "Happy now?" she snarled at her phone as she stomped on the gas to propel the vehicle up the grassy verge back onto the gravel road.

"In one. Hundred. Metres. Your destination. Will be. On the left," Google Maps cheerfully said.

"Gnnngh!"

Nina drove back the way she came. There really was nothing there, only scraggly bushes with branches sticking out in all directions.

But wait! What was that?

Nina slammed on the brakes.

"You. Have arrived at. Your destination!" the navigator announced jubilantly.

There was an opening in that hedge. Hidden between long scraggly branches, nearly swallowed up by the greenery on either side, was a gate. A picket gate of sorts, which might once have been painted white.

Her fingers suddenly shaking, Nina pulled to the side of the road, turned off the ignition and unfastened her seat belt.

"You. Have arrived at—"

Nina grabbed the phone off the dash of the car and stabbed her finger at the "off" button.

"I told you to shut up," she said and shoved the phone into her purse with more violence that was strictly necessary. There was something about that gate—something almost familiar, but at the same time tantalizingly mysterious.

In the sudden silence, Nina could hear her heart beating, and she sat with her hand clutching the door handle for what seemed like an eternity.

What was she doing here? Had she taken complete leave of her senses? What was a big-city girl with a good job and a nice apartment in Vancouver doing in backwoods BC, looking for a cottage left to her by a person she had never even heard of until this person's lawyer tracked her down at her place of work?

"We received these documents quite recently," James Spreckles, the surprisingly young lawyer, had said to Nina. "It appears that they'd been left with instructions that they were to be forwarded to us in June of this year—is there any special significance to this date?"

"Not that I can think of," Nina had said, "other than the fact that I turned thirty in June."

"Ah," he said. "That might be why. We apologize for not getting them to you earlier, but we had some difficulty finding you. Hence the somewhat unusual, uh, course of action."

He then proceeded to lay a sheaf of paperwork in front of Nina, and when she had signed her name about a dozen times, he'd stuffed several of them in an envelope and handed them to her. He then shook her hand, congratulating her on her new property, and with a look at his watch that told Nina he was a very busy person, and already running late for something, ushered her out the door.

2557 Hawthorn Lane, Houghton, BC, said the street address on the title deed. Nina had never been out to that corner of the province. She should at least take a look... So she had tossed some clothes into her little suitcase, punched the address into Google Maps, and set out. And spent the last several hours driving over lonely country highways, surrounded by nothing but mountains and trees, wondering what mad impulse had possessed her. Was this whole thing really real?

Nina gave herself a mental push and opened the car door. The dark green leaves of the hedge bristled at her from across the street. So what? She could tackle a hedge, yes indeed! Nina swung her feet out of the car, pushing down the automatic door lock button out of sheer habit, then stood up and slammed the door shut behind her.

Aaaack! She whirled around and frantically tugged on the car door handle. No no no no no no! It was locked, solidly locked! So was the passenger side door, and the trunk, and no amount of tugging and rattling at the door handles made any difference. How could she be so stupid? Of all the times... The key was in the ignition, grinning at her in her despair, and of course there was her purse, on the passenger seat. With her phone in it, and the spare key she always carried in her wallet for exactly such an eventuality. Nina dug in her pants pocket—did she have something, anything, to jimmy the lock? Didn't the BCAA people use some kind of flat piece of metal to do the job?

Her fingers closed on something flat and metallic in her pocket. A key? A flicker of hope flared up, and she whipped the thing out of her pocket. But no, it wasn't the spare car key. It was a key all right, but a house key, an old-fashioned rounded key in a brassy colour, a little bit rusted, with a ring at the top, a cylindrical shaft and some teeth sticking out at the bottom.

A house key? Uncomprehendingly, Nina stared at it for a second, then memory penetrated her panic-addled brain. It was the key to the cottage, of course, which, according to Google Maps (now locked in the car), was behind that tall bristly hedge staring at her from across the street. The lawyer had given the key to her along with all that paperwork, and she must have shoved it into her pants pocket without thinking.

Well, at least she wasn't completely stuck. Maybe there was a phone in that house—just maybe? Then she could call BCAA and get someone to come out to help her.

So. Nina squared her shoulders and determinedly walked across the street to the gate hidden in the hedge.

It was made of narrow slats of wood some five feet high, its once-white paint peeling off in thin strips. The branches closed in the sides and arched over top, reaching for Nina. Yikes, there were thorns on those branches! Carefully, Nina reached out and pushed at the gate. To her surprise, it gently swung open with a little creak. Nina peered through the opening. A tangle of greenery met her eye. Grasses, shrubs, bushes, and tree limbs obscured her vision, but behind them, she could see the pale grey of weathered cedar siding, and a path of flagstones disappeared into the tangle, going in the direction of the house.

Nina turned sideways, sucked in her stomach to make herself as narrow as possible, and sidled through the opening. A thorn snagged her T-shirt, but it let go again immediately—almost as if it was plucking at her sleeve in a friendly greeting. Nina looked around, and she saw that the gate had silently swung closed behind her. She bit her lip. Then she raised her chin and turned to follow the flagstone path, weaving through the thicket of growth. Pink, yellow and white spikes of hollyhock, taller than Nina herself, grew beside and on the path, clumps of yellow-centred white daisies around their feet; long tendrils of purple clematis and pale blue morning glory wound up the trunk of a tree. The whole garden seemed alive—there was a soft rustling and humming in the undergrowth and little chirps and tweets of birds; then a chipmunk darted across Nina's path. It froze momentarily when it caught sight of her, tilted its head inquiringly, twitched up the hazelnut it had in its paws as if it was offering to share, then scurried on into the rustling grasses.

Nina went closer to the house. It had a front porch whose posts were covered in grapevines climbing up and around and from there onto the roof; clusters of tiny green grapes dangled down like earrings from a giantess' earlobes. To the right of the front door stood a well-used wicker rocking chair with a little weathered table beside it; against the wall were stacked a couple of wooden crates. The cedar siding of the house had gone silvery-grey with age, the white-painted window frames shining against it.

Nina lifted her foot to step on the bottom step of the porch, then stopped. This place was so old, her foot might go right through the boards! Then again, there was no rot that she could see—it actually looked remarkably solid. Cautiously she put her weight onto the step. There was a little creak, then nothing; the stairs were as firm as those in her apartment building in Vancouver.

With a sigh of relief, Nina climbed the rest of the stairs onto the porch. She took the key from her pocket, and, with her heart beating high in her throat, fitted it into the keyhole of the front door. A little bit of wiggling, and the lock clicked back. Slowly she pushed open the door and stepped over the threshold.

The stale air of a house that has stood empty for a long time hit Nina's nostrils. She looked around. The front door opened directly into the living room, which was panelled in a fawn-coloured wood. To the right, a couch, upholstered in a brown nineteen-seventies plaid, flanked a fireplace, with a wooden crate in front of it that served as a coffee table; opposite, faded blue curtains draped a pair of French doors, through which Nina could see more of the tangle that was the garden. On the left, an open doorway led into another room. Nina looked around the door post. It was the kitchen, with arborite-topped counters over dark oak cabinets, a table with three spindle-leg chairs, and a stove against the wall. The cook top didn't have normal coil burners, but some weird grille things on the top—a gas stove, perhaps? In the corner of the kitchen stood a harvest gold fridge of the same vintage as the plaid living room couch, and a white porcelain sink was mounted under the window that looked out onto the garden tangle.

A beige rotary phone was attached to the wall beside the doorway. A phone! Nina snatched the receiver off its hook and held it to her ear.

Silence.

Well, of course, it would be too much to ask to still have the phone connected...

But what about power? The place was wired for electricity, or there wouldn't be a fridge. And there was the light switch next to the phone. She flicked it up and down.

Nothing. That figured.

So, no power, no phone. She vaguely remembered from looking at Google Maps that some kind of small town was a little ways down the road, but she hadn't paid attention to the distance. Was it walkable?

But actually, the first thing she needed was a bathroom. Oh, but did the water still work? Or would she have to go outside and squat in the bushes?

There was only one way to find out. Nina cranked the tap on the sink. A clanking and creaking noise came from the pipes, a groan like a soul in agony—and then a gush of thick, rust-coloured, metallic-smelling liquid poured into the sink.

"Oy!" Nina turned the tap off again. "Well, at least it's liquid... I think." She turned the tap back on, and this time it started pouring without its strange noises; the colour was noticeably lighter. "Hmm," she said, "just need to flush it out, do we?" She let the water run for a bit until it had become the colour of very weak tea. "Well, that's good. So there's hope."

She found the bathroom down the hall. It contained an old-fashioned clawfoot tub, a sink whose dial taps looked like little crosses, and—thank goodness!—a toilet. Its tank was mounted high up on the wall at the level of Nina's head, a chain with a small ceramic club at the end of it—presumably a handle—hanging from the side. There was a flaky rust-brown stain in the bottom of the toilet bowl where the water had dried up. Nina took hold of the ceramic thing and pulled. The creaks and clanks were even more gruesome than in the kitchen, but with an enormous groan, a small amount of liquid rust poured into the toilet bowl.

"Yes!" Nina punched her fist in the air. "Success!"

The House

The strange thing about the house was in how good a shape it was. Judging by the rust coming out of the pipes and the smell of long disuse, not to mention the jungle outside, it had to have stood empty for years. But other than the rust there was no sign of decay—no mouse droppings, no birds' nests in the fireplace, barely even any dust.

Across the hall from the bathroom Nina pushed down an ornate cast iron door handle, and with a soft creak the door opened on a bedroom. The wide wooden bedstead in the middle under the window was covered with a patchwork quilt in a "wedding ring" pattern. Just like Granny used to have—even the same colours as Granny's: soft blues, moss greens, and dusty pinks on a beige ground. The curtains on the window picked up the moss green, and a multi-coloured rag rug on the floor provided another splash of colour.

Nina gave the quilt a little tap, but to her surprise, the dust cloud she had expected didn't materialize. She held her breath and pinched her nose, then gave the blanket a harder slap, but there was no more dust than when she had made her bed that morning back in her apartment in Vancouver. Curious. Nina ran her finger over the white-painted dresser that stood beside the bed, and it, too, was perfectly clean.

A honey-coloured taper candle in a brass candle holder stood on top of the dresser, a little box of matches lying beside it. The bedside table had a small standing lamp on it—Nina tried the switch, just to be sure, but of course nothing happened—and on the other side of the bed was a bookcase full of books. Nina wandered over to take a look. Classics, mostly, many of them paperbacks with covers that looked like they were from the seventies or eighties: *Pride and Prejudice*, some Agatha Christie, Jules Verne, *The Princess and the Goblin*, a fat volume of Grimm's *Children's and Household Tales*, another of the collected edition of Shakespeare, some Dickens, *The Wonderful Wizard of Oz*, *The Adventures of Sherlock Holmes*, and a few other novels Nina didn't recognize. Apparently this Miranda lady liked old stories.

The books were the most personal thing Nina had found in the house yet—otherwise, there was very little indication of the previous owner. No photos, no personal papers...

Nina wandered back towards the living room, and she realized that she was hungry. Food. She had some protein bars in her purse, she'd have to get—oh shoot. The purse was locked in the car. And as of this moment, she had no way to get the car unlocked, to call BCAA and get herself sorted out. The town, where there might be a phone, was who-knew-how-far, and even if there was a grocery store or even just a gas station that sold food, her bank card and cash were securely locked in the car inside her wallet. So... was there anything left in this house that one could eat? Maybe Miranda had left some cans of pork and beans. Those things lasted forever, didn't they?

She pulled open one of the oak cupboard doors. Dishes. Thick, white stoneware mugs with blue rims, matching plates of various sizes, soup bowls. A wooden thing with a metal crank handle on the top that Nina recognized from watching the *Antiques Roadshow*—wasn't it a manual coffee grinder? Sure enough, the small drawer in the bottom still smelled faintly of coffee. So, if this was the dish cupboard, the drawer underneath probably had cutlery, right? Right. The cupboard below that was stocked with pots and pans.

So, the next one over? Nina struck pay dirt. There weren't just one or two cans of baked beans—that cupboard was *full.* Beans, tuna, glass jars with what looked like home-canned produce—were those peaches?—jam, sugar, salt, spices, a sealed container of oatmeal, and another one of powdered milk. On the top shelf was a fancy tin, one of those black and red and gold Chinese ones. Nina popped off the lid. It was tea! And not only that, it smelled perfectly all right. Now if she only had power to put on the kettle, a cup of tea would exactly hit the spot. But power there was none...

Experimentally, not expecting anything to happen, Nina turned one of the knobs on the stove—and she jumped back in surprise. The front burner leapt to life! The gas was still working? That was fantastic—she could have that cup of tea! And perhaps even heat up a can of beans.

After a few minutes of rummaging, she had found a tea kettle—the kind with the spout that whistled when the water came to a boil—a tea pot, a strainer, a can opener, a saucepan and a wooden spoon, and she was trying to keep the pork and beans from burning in the bottom of the pot. She remembered how, when Granny first switched from an electric range to a gas one, back when Nina was a little girl, her first few meals all burned—gas heated up so much faster than electricity.

By the time she sat on the non-dusty couch with her cup of tea and bowl of baked beans, it was starting to get dark outside. Drat. Too late to go for that walk to the next town in search of help. Not that she actually knew how to get there in the first place—finding the cottage had involved turning on little side streets that she would never have noticed without Google Maps; she'd probably get hopelessly lost in the woods out there without it. The only thing left to do was to find something to jimmy the lock of the car door herself—and she'd have to do it now, before it got too dark to see.

A more exhaustive search of the kitchen cupboards yielded nothing more useful than a long knife, and Nina didn't think that fishing around in the door of her Toyota with a butcher knife would be a good idea. And didn't a slim jim have a hook on the end for pulling up the knob, anyway?

A rummage around the bathroom didn't turn up anything more useful, either. There was toilet paper in the cupboard under the sink, and the drawer was empty of everything but a comb, a still-wrapped toothbrush, and a cake of Ivory soap.

Nina moved on to the bedroom. There was a pair of louvred closet doors that she hadn't looked behind yet. She pulled them open and took a step back in surprise: there were clothes still on the hangers—half a dozen or so soft long dresses, skirts and blouses, in some indeterminate classic style that didn't come from any particular decade that Nina recognized. She ran her hand along the row of garments, half expecting to dislodge a few moths, but the outfits just softly swayed on their hangers, releasing a faint scent of long-forgotten lavender sachets. Wait—hangers! Couldn't you jimmy a lock with a bent coat hanger? But on closer inspection, these ones wouldn't do—not a single cheap wire hanger among the lot; they were all solid wooden ones.

Nina turned to the dresser in the corner. If there were still clothes in the closet, what about the dresser? Sure enough, the top drawer held a couple of pretty nightgowns—actual nightgowns!—with ruching along the neckline, and even some bloomer-style pants to match, while the next one down had cotton stockings and warm socks. The lowest drawer yielded a couple of pairs of bib-front twill overalls with grass-stained knees.

It was getting harder to see in the gathering dusk. Nina shrugged. There wasn't much point in trying to keep up the search tonight. Her eye fell on the candle and matches on top of the dresser. Well, why not? She'd need some kind of light.

Wrapped in the quilt from the bed, the last cup of tea at her elbow, she curled up on the couch with *Pride and Prejudice.* It seemed an apt read by candlelight. She felt oddly comfortable in this house—safe, as if this was where she belonged. She almost regretted that she would have to set out on that hike in the morning to find help for getting into her car... she liked this house...

Charlie

A sliver of bright morning sun fell through the chink in the curtains and right over Nina's face, waking her. She stirred, sneezed and stretched. Slowly she came conscious to the feel of the quilt over top of her and the linen sheets under her, and as she did so, the memory of yesterday woke as well. The cottage, her locked car—and she was sleeping in an old-fashioned bed wearing an even more old-fashioned white cotton nightgown, which, considering it was a stranger's, fitted her surprisingly well.

Nina sat up and looked around the room. Her jeans and the T-shirt she had worn yesterday were draped over the bedpost where she had hung them last night; the candle on the bedside table was burned down to a stump. *Pride and Prejudice* had held her spellbound until deep into the night. She didn't really know how late, as her only timepiece was her phone, securely locked inside her car. She'd forgotten how riveting the story of Elizabeth and Mr

Darcy was—forgotten, or never known. A while ago she had watched the movie on Netflix, but there, the tale was over in a couple of hours, unlike the book, which allowed you to revel in the story, live in that world, until the bedside candle burned down and the book kept dropping from your hands because you simply couldn't keep your eyes open any longer.

Nina pulled aside the curtain over the head of the bed and looked out. There was that tangle of garden outside, so thick you could hardly tell what was what. A tall section of grass that might have been a lawn once, scattered with flowers of all colours and descriptions, was interspersed with some small pine trees that looked like they had sprung up there on their own, and some kind of maple—no more than a sapling. And there, what was that in the corner of the yard? Another building?

Half an hour later she stood with a mug of tea in her hand outside the French doors on what had once been a patio. Pinky-beige flagstones lay underfoot, clumps of grass and tiny flowers growing in the cracks. Some chest-high bushes had encroached on the space, crowding nearly to the doors, lifting the patio stones in places and cracking them in others, but Nina could see where there had once been a set of steps leading off the patio further out into the garden.

She pushed her way through the bushes, carefully avoiding the clusters of shiny black berries that dangled enticingly from the branches. She didn't know enough about plants to trust these ones. For all she knew, they were deadly nightshade; she'd heard somewhere that those were black. Beyond the bushes, she found—more bushes. Waist-high grass, with other, weedy-looking things in between. Determinedly, Nina pushed on. You'd need a machete to get through this, she thought. Maybe there was one in that shed—she was sure it was a shed—in the corner of the yard?

The garden rustled and hummed around Nina. A big bush of wild roses buzzed with bees, birds chirped and fluttered up and away as Nina passed, and her chipmunk friend from yesterday ran along beside her on a tree branch.

"No nuts this time?" Nina asked the chipmunk. He tilted his head quizzically, chittered at her, then scurried off up the trunk of the tree. "Fine then," Nina called after him, "but next time I want my share!"

The chipmunk scolded down at her, and she laughed. What a glorious day! And what a wonderful, mysterious garden, in spite of—or perhaps because of—the huge tangle it was in. Nina still didn't know how she was going to get into her car, or into town to make a phone call to get BCAA to come help her, but somehow it didn't matter so much at the moment. And maybe there'd be some tool in that shed that could make it happen?

Her foot caught on something and she stumbled. It was a protruding wooden frame, about a foot high, coming apart at the corners. And spilling out of it in between all the grasses and bushes were—strawberries! Nina recognized strawberries. Even a city girl who bought her produce at the supermarket knew what those were, and she'd never heard of any toxic lookalikes to beware of. Gleefully, she plucked a berry off the plant, twisted out the little stem, and popped it in her mouth. Her eyes blinked open in surprise. It was a full-on taste explosion; she had never experienced a strawberry as sweet and at the same time as flavourful as this. She picked another one to test if the effect was the same—it was. Mmmh, amazing.

Next to the strawberries was a patch of lacy greenery, rather like the asparagus fern her grandmother used to have in a pot in the corner of the living room. Nina brushed her fingers through the greens—but wait, she recognized this, too! She squatted down and peered more closely at the bottom of the plants. Sure enough, there was a little orange bump where the greenery came out of the ground—she was right, they were carrots! She gave an experimental tug on one of the plants. A stubby, four-inch-long carrot popped out of the ground, dirt clinging to its sides.

"Will you look at that!" Nina said. She pulled on another carrot, but it didn't want to come up—the greens broke off right at the top of the root. "Hmph," she said and tugged on the one that grew directly next to it—practically on top of it, in fact. She wiggled it back and forth in the ground a bit before pulling up—there, now it was looser, and the broken-off one was wiggling as well. She dug her fingers in around the neck of the carrot, and pulled. Both of them came up together.

"Ah, that's why you didn't want to come up," she said. The two carrots were intertwined, one wrapped around the other like a pair of corkscrews. "What do you know—Frankencarrot!" Nina shook the dirt off the orange roots. "Hmm, is there water to wash you off with?" She stood up, stretched on tiptoe and slewed her head around. Ah, there, by the corner of the shed, that looked like a barrel full of water! She wiggled, pushed and wended her way through the tangle of vegetables, grass, and weeds, narrowly avoided tripping over more of the broken wooden boxes—they'd probably been raised garden beds at some point—and made her way to the container by the shed. It was a big metal barrel, blue paint peeling off its sides, brimful of clean, clear water.

"Hmm." She dunked her carrots in the water, scrubbed the dirt off with her hands, then bit the end of one of them. "Oh wow!" Crunchy, so sweet, a little bit earthy, yet somehow *clear*—if a flavour could be called that...

"A garden full of good things to eat..." she murmured quietly to herself. "Carrots and strawberries and lettuces... There! Those are lettuces, aren't they?" There were clumps of bright green frilly leaves mixed in with smooth-edged deep purplish-red ones, and some that looked like the Romaine lettuce Nina sometimes bought at the store. She picked the tip off one of the leaves and gingerly tasted it. Yes, that was lettuce all right. And there, that looked like parsley, the tightly-curled frilly kind they put on plates in restaurants as garnish, and next to it clumps of something like green onions. Except they had clusters of little bulbs at the top, similar to heads of garlic that had split into individual cloves. She picked one off and smelled it. Definitely onion of some kind. Green onions with their seeds growing at the top of the stalk, perhaps? Lettuce and green onions and carrots—she could already see the salad she could make out of all those. Hadn't there been some vinegar in the kitchen cupboard? Maybe even some oil.

In a tangle behind the green onions was a bush with dark green heart-shaped leaves with purple veins and small dark purple flowers; in between hung slender, deep purple pods about three or four inches long. Except for the colour, they looked like beans. But beans in purple? Nina didn't trust those. However, now that she looked closer, she saw that there were some green pods in that tangle as well, on vines that had bright red flowers. Scarlet runner beans—the name popped into her head. She didn't know where she'd heard it before—maybe Granny again?

This garden was a profusion of colour. All the different shades of green, flowers in white and sunshine yellow and bright orange, the deep purples and scarlets of those bean flowers—and closing the colour wheel were some beautiful little star-shaped flowers in a cerulean blue, like the sky on a crisp fall day. They grew on two-foot high stalks with fleshy pale green leaves with small hairs standing up on them. Nina bent down to touch one, to see if it was as prickly as it looked.

"They taste like cucumbers, you know," a male voice came from Nina's right.

With a scream, Nina whirled around.

Against the trunk of a gnarly tree, whose branches were loaded with tiny apples, leaned a man. He had his arms crossed over his broad chest, a red-checked flannel lumberjacket gaping open over a black T-shirt. With his scruffy brown beard, heavy boots, and work-stained jeans he looked like he had come off a construction site.

"Sheesh, you scared me!" Nina said, her hand to her heart. What was he doing here?

"Sorry about that," the man said with a smile, which lit up his astonishingly blue eyes. "Didn't mean to freak you out." He pushed himself away from the tree trunk, stepped over to Nina and held out his hand. "Charlie Hayward," he said.

"Uh—okay." Nina took his hand, then dropped it again quickly. "Where did you come from?"

"Oh, uh, I, uh, live around here," he said, tilting his head vaguely in the direction of the thick forest that started behind the shed.

"I didn't know there are houses back there," Nina said. Actually, she didn't know anything about this place, so that didn't mean much. "Uh, what can I do for you?"

He smiled again. "I thought I'd drop by, see if there was anything *I* could do for *you*," he said. "Explain the vegetables, maybe? If you can find them in this mess." He critically inspected the tangle of greenery around his feet, then took hold of one of the purple vines and pulled it upwards. "For example," he said, gesturing at it with his other hand, "meet purple runner bean. Purple runner bean, meet lovely lady without a name."

In spite of herself Nina chuckled. "So that *is* a bean, is it? I was wondering."

"Oh yes, it's a perfectly legitimate bean," he said, "just a little flamboyant in its clothing habits. Once it gets into hot water, it drops its pretense though."

Nina wrinkled her forehead.

"When it's cooked, it turns green like every other string bean," he translated.

"Ah," Nina said.

"Now here," he said, pulling up another one of the bean vines, "is a humble scarlet—"

"Runner bean, I know," Nina said smugly.

"Yes, quite right!" He let the vine drop back into the tangle. "Have you yet made the acquaintance of borage?" He bent down and picked one of the sky-blue flowers. "As I was trying to point out when I so rudely made you jump out of your skin, the leaves taste of cucumber." He pulled one of the large leaves off the plant and bit the end off it. "Would you care for a taste?" With a bow, he held the flower out to Nina.

She laughed. "You're weird, you know," she said.

"I aim to please," he replied. "Do try, it's worth it. You could also freeze the flowers in ice cube trays and decoratively float them in drinks with little paper umbrellas."

"Oh, all right then," Nina said. She picked the end off one of the leaves, put it in her mouth and chewed it. The fuzzy prickles made for a strange sensation in the mouth, but once you got past that, it did indeed taste like cucumber.

"Interesting," she said.

"It is indeed," he said. "There are any number of interesting vegetables in this garden."

"So—what's this garden to you?" Nina asked. "Are you a neighbour? Come here often?"

"I've kind of kept an eye on things a bit," he said. "So, what brings you here?"

"I'm not entirely sure," Nina replied, scratching her head. "I got this letter..." Wait, why was she telling this total stranger her life story? This was not a good idea, not a good idea at all. "Well, actually—" she said, hedging.

"Yes?"

"You did say you wanted to help me out, yes?"

"Yes indeed." He had a trace of an accent—Australian, British, something like that.

"Well, I locked myself out of my car. Could I use your cell phone to call BCAA?"

"Haven't got one, I'm afraid," he said with an apologetic grin.

"Haven't got one? What century are you living in?" Nina smiled as she said it—she didn't exactly want to offend the guy.

He smiled back. "The late 20th, pretty much."

Nina huffed. "There goes that idea. Well, I couldn't find anything like a slim jim to break into the car—not that I'd know how to use it, anyway. If you don't have a cell phone, do you have one of those handy? Or do you know if there's one around somewhere, or a wire coat hanger, or anything like that?"

"The shed might have something useful," he said, and he climbed over the bean tangle and started wading in the direction of the garden shed.

"What's in there, anyway?" Nina carefully stepped after him through the tangle of greenery. "Oh, look," she exclaimed, "there's a tomato!"

"That would be an Early Girl," he said, picking the round red fruit of the vine. "So called because, well, they're early." He held it out to Nina. "There are lots of others coming later in the season."

"You seem to know your way around this garden pretty well," Nina said. "What's the deal?" She smelled the tomato, decided that it seemed pretty safe, and took a bite. Another flavour explosion detonated in her mouth. "Oh my gosh!" she exclaimed around a mouthful of tomato. "Thish ish amashing!"

"Not bad, eh?" He reached the shed and started wiggling the handle of the door up and down. "Early Girls aren't the best tomato variety there is, but because they're the first, they're always one of the most enjoyable. By the end of August, your palate gets jaded and no longer appreciates the finer points of tomato-ness." His wiggling of the handle seemed to have loosened the door from where it was stuck, and with a sharp tug, he pulled it open.

Nina swallowed the last piece of the Early Girl. "The finer points of tom-ah-to-ness," she echoed. "I certainly didn't appreciate them before. Also, you didn't answer my question," she said, stepping up behind him to look over his shoulder into the inside of the shed.

"Which question was that?" He walked into the dim interior of the shed. A faint light came through the very grimy panes of a window on the right, dimly illuminating what looked like a couple of work benches and a few dark outlines of something-or-other stacked on top of them. He grabbed a rag from the top of one of the benches and wiped at the window panes with it. The light got a bit brighter, and Nina looked around the shed. It was old and dilapidated, paint peeling off the window frames, exposing weathered wood cracked with age. A large water stain ran down the wall underneath the window behind the rusty implements that hung on hooks above the workbench. Nina recognized pliers, a thing that looked like a saw, a hammer... She stepped around Charlie.

"Hey, you're right, this might have something that'll work!" She peered at the rusty tools. "I don't see any screwdrivers though. I wonder..." There were a couple of drawers beneath the top of the work bench. Nina tugged on the rust-darkened handle of the one on the left, and it came off in her hand. "Hmph," she said, and reached out for the other one. Her hand sank into a mass of cobwebs.

"Eeeek!" She jumped back, tripped on something, stumbled and fell backwards onto her butt, crashing into a stack of items that fell over with a metallic clatter. "Aaah!" she yelled. A small creature skittered out from underneath the stack of whatever-it-was that had fallen over and ran off. Nina scrabbled to her feet with a little scream and scuttled back out of the shed, beating at her arms and rear to brush off whatever it was she had picked up in there, and shaking herself all over. "Yuck!" she said finally, when she had calmed down a bit. "That's—yikes, it's creepy in there!"

There was no reply.

Nina looked around. Where had the Charlie guy gone? She spun in a full circle, but she couldn't see him anywhere.

"Hey! Hello? Where'd you go? Hellooooo?"

Nothing.

That was weird—he seemed to have vanished.

Ah well. Nina shrugged. He'd showed up out of the blue, then disappeared back into the blue. Playing the mystery man, was he? Fine, two could play at that game—or not play it, as it were. She wasn't going to go hunting for the guy.

However, she still didn't have anything to get into her car with. There was nothing else for it: she'd have to go back into that scary shed. She carefully stepped over the threshold, pulling in her head and keeping her arms as close to her sides as possible. Eew—she'd have to touch that drawer handle again! So not nice, so not nice... She stretched out a finger, barely touched, then whipped it back again and shuddered. Eeew eeew eeew! Nina *so* did not love cobwebs.

Actually, maybe if she got a tool, like a stick or something of that sort... She stepped outside and found a thin, whippy branch with a few leaves still clinging on it. That ought to do. She shoved the stick into the drawer handle, twisted it about a bit to wipe up most of the cobwebs, then pulled it back out and tossed it as far out the door as it would go, hoping that any remaining spiders went with it. And there was the cloth that Charlie—if that was actually his name—had used to wipe the window. She picked it up with two fingers, shook it out, and used it to wipe down the drawer handle one more time. Then a pull. It wouldn't budge. She tried again, wiggling and yanking. The whole workbench shook, rattling the tools hung on the backboard. But there—hadn't it budged a little? Nina was sure it had moved. She yanked again, and with a grating noise, the drawer came out a bit.

"Come—out—of—there!" Nina said through gritted teeth with yank after yank. A pair of pliers popped off its hook on the back of the work bench, then a hammer followed, clattering onto the work surface. But one more yank should do it! There was stuff rattling around in there, and she was going to get at it. "Come—on!" One more mighty pull, and it finally budged. With a groaning, grating noise, the drawer came open another handsbreadth, and sure enough, there were some long things with handles in there. Screwdrivers?

Nina shook out the cloth one more time, then wrapped it around her hand and fished in the drawer. Out came what looked like a screwdriver, but it didn't have the flat end that Nina was looking for; it had a square tip.

"What the heck is that?" Nina said, peering at it at arm's length.

"It's a Robertson driver," Charlie's voice said from behind her.

She jumped.

"Will you quit *doing* that?" she said, irritated, and turned around, only to find his face no more than a few inches from her own. She backed up against the work bench, leaning back to create some space between them.

"I'm sorry," he said and took a step backwards, bumping into the pile of metal stuff Nina had knocked over earlier. "Whoa!" He staggered, flung out an arm to steady himself, crashed into the edge of a shelf, tipped it, and sent a stack of small flower pots raining down on his head. "Yow, ow, ouch!" He ducked, trying to protect himself from the flying missiles with his arms thrown over his head. Then just as the cascade ceased and he lowered his arms, one last pot came down, dumping a load of potting soil down his shirt collar. He gave a yelp.

Nina burst out laughing.

Charlie clawed at his neck, trying to get the dirt out from under his collar, shaking himself all over, then he chuckled.

"I guess it's funny if it happens to someone else," he said. "There, I've been punished for startling you—again. So will you forgive me?"

"All right." Nina held out the thing in her hand. "So that's a screwdriver?"

"Yes, a Robertson driver. A red Robertson, by the looks of it. Come on, you're Canadian, don't you know what a Robertson screwdriver is?"

Nina looked at the screwdriver. "It's not red," she said.

"No, not that particular one," he replied. "But if they're standardized, they are. The ones for Number Eight screws usually have red handles."

"Do they now," Nina said. "And that's significant how?" She stepped out of the shed—it was getting a bit crowded in there.

Charlie came after her, still trying to shake the dirt out of his shirt collar. "Hmph," he grunted, then he shrugged out of his mac jacket and shook it with a snap, scattering dirt. "It's not significant," he said, dropping the jacket on a tall bushy plant with clusters of bright red, slightly dried-up looking berries. "I simply thought,"—he reached behind his head and grabbed the back of his T-shirt collar—"that seeing as you asked what it was, I'd give you a proper answer." The last part of the sentence came out muffled as his face disappeared in the T-shirt he was pulling up over his head, exposing a muscular chest with a mat of curly hairs.

Nina raised her eyebrows. "Uh..." She felt her face warm up.

His face came back out from under the T-shirt, and he saw the look on her face. "Oh, uh, sorry. Trying to, you know—" He shook out the T-shirt, then pulled it back over his head backwards. "Damn—um..." He repeated the manoeuvre of pulling the shirt off, turned it around and put it back on. By the time his head emerged from the shirt, his curly hair was all over the place and his face looked flushed. He wiggled his shoulders a bit to dislodge the last of the dirt, then fished his red flannel shirt back off the bush. He gave Nina a glance out of the corner of his eye as he shrugged back into the jacket. "So, is the red Robby going to be any good for you?"

Nina glanced down at the screwdriver in her hand. "No," she said, "not really. Unless you know a technique for getting a locked car door open with this thing."

He laughed. "No, not particularly," he said. "What kind of car is it?"

"A Toyota Corolla. One of the small ones. A bit older; it's a 2011."

He did a tiny double-take. "2011—older?"

"Yes? That's twelve years old."

"Oh." He was silent for a moment, and an undefinable look crossed his face. Then he looked at his watch, an old-fashioned analog one. "Oh, damn, it stopped. What is it today?" He gave his head a small shake. "I mean, do you have the time?"

Nina shook her head. "'Fraid not. I don't wear a watch anymore, just use my phone. And *that*, I'm afraid, is locked inside my car. Hence, this." She wiggled the screwdriver in her hand. "But I guess if that one doesn't do me any good, well..."

He squared his shoulders, put on a heroic expression and held out his hand for the screwdriver. "Fear not, fair maiden. Entrust to me the task of finding a weapon to conquer your difficulties."

Nina snorted. "I'm cast for the damsel in distress, am I?" She clapped the screwdriver into his hand. "I'd be offended, if I wasn't actually in a tight spot here. Go slay me a dragon, Sir Knight—or get me a slim jim, that would be more useful."

He took the screwdriver and wandered back into the shed.

"Incidentally," Nina said from the safety of the doorway, "how far is town from here?"

"What, Houghton? Oh, about five miles thataway." He waved his left hand with another screwdriver in some unspecific direction behind Nina's head.

"Five miles? That's, like, eight kilometres, isn't it?" Nina was appalled. That was way too far to walk, especially in her sandals—which was all she had for footwear; her runners were, of course, in the car. "And I don't even know how to get there... You don't have Google Maps on your—oh yeah, you don't have a cell phone." She wrinkled her nose. "Can you give me directions? Or, actually—could you give me a ride?" He had to have a car, else how could he live out here in the boondocks?

"Uh, my truck is out of commission at the moment," he said, "but here, is this the sort of thing you're looking for?" He emerged from the shed with a rusty strip of metal.

Nina grabbed it from his hand. "Yes!" She turned it around a few times. "What is it?"

"It was a ruler, once upon a time."

"Great, that ought to do it. Maybe. At least that's what the BCAA lady had last time this happened... Or something like it, anyway. Let's give it a shot."

She turned around and waded through the thicket towards the house.

"You can go around the side, you know," Charlie said.

"Yes, I suppose you can."

The side of the house was just as much of a tangle of growth as the back yard. There was a leaning post with a rusty old pulley for a clothesline that had probably once been connected to the house on the other end; more trees with small green fruits on them—apples? peaches?—and a snarl of vines with small greenish berries that looked like raspberries. "Raspberries? Aren't they supposed to be finished by now?"

"Those aren't raspberries, they're blackberries." Charlie was right behind her. "They're not ready until the end of August or so. The raspberries are over... over there, by the fence." He pointed off in the direction away from the house.

"Oh, there's a fence behind all that stuff?"

"Yes, usually."

Usually? That was kind of weird. It sounded as if he knew this garden, had known it when it wasn't all tangled and messy.

Nina brushed against a plant with grey-green fleshy leaves, and a sharp scent rose from it.

"Oh! What's this?"

"The herb patch," Charlie said. "Sage; in this case, common or garden. Somewhere—oh yeah, here. That's variegated sage." He pointed out another plant, nearly smothered in grass and weeds, that had similar leaves, except they were patterned in silver and purple as well as the grey-green. "And golden sage here,"—that one had a yellow-green centre to each leaf—"and pineapple sage." He picked a leaf off the last plant, crushed it between his fingers and held it under Nina's nose. It had a strong, not unpleasant scent, a cross between something fruity and, well, turkey stuffing.

"Nice," Nina said, "what could you use it for, I wonder? Chicken?"

Charlie gave an affirmative grunt. "That's usually what Mir—" He broke off.

Nina spun around. "What who?"

He looked aside.

"And what's with the 'usually'? What *are* you actually doing here? What's your connection with this place?"

"I told you," he said, "neighbour." He looked a bit shifty as he said it.

"So, you must have been here a long time then, if you knew all about this garden before it got so messy," Nina said accusingly. He wasn't old enough to have lived here for a long time, though. Unless... "Did you grow up here?"

He shrugged. "No, I didn't. Look, this is lemon thyme," he said, bending down and running his hand over a carpet of tiny yellow-green leaves. "I like the smell of it." A scent like lemon peel wafted up to Nina's nose.

"Yeah, that's nice. You didn't answer my question about what you're doing here."

There was a chittering sound, and Charlie crouched down.

"Hey, Felix!" he said, holding out his hand. Nina's chipmunk came scurrying out of the grass towards him, stopped with its tail and nose twitching simultaneously, and sniffed his fingers.

"Felix, huh? Why Felix?"

"All chipmunks are called Felix, didn't you know that?" Charlie looked up at her, a twinkle lighting up his blue eyes.

Nina rolled her eyes. "Oh, they are, are they?"

"Well, in reality it's squirrels that are called Felix—the red European ones. But you don't have them around here, so chipmunks have to fill the Felix role." He rose from his crouch and watched the chipmunk skittering away into the grasses. "This one is a good friend of mine."

"Uh-huh," Nina said skeptically. "He's promiscuous—he was hitting on me yesterday, too. *And* this morning."

"Can't say I blame him," Charlie said, giving Nina a sidelong glance.

"Ex*cuse* me?"

He chuckled. "Sorry," he said with a grin. "Won't happen again."

"Hmph!" Nina slapped her palm with the metal ruler. "Okay, let's try this thing. I've got to get into that car of mine. Oh, look—I didn't realize we'd got as far around the house as this already; that has to be the bedroom window."

"Yup," Charlie grunted behind her.

He knew the inside of the house, too, did he?

Nina pushed her way through the tangle of grasses and bushes and came out on the flagstone path by the front door of the cottage. She could hear the rustle and cracks of Charlie's movement behind her.

"So, if you've been here this long," she said, reaching the gate grown into the hedge, "you must know who this person was who used to live here!" He'd pretty much said as much, earlier—she was sure he'd been about to say something about "Miranda," before he broke off. "Who was she?" She reached for the handle of the gate and pulled it open, looking around to see the expression on Charlie's face as he answered her question.

He was gone.

Stuck

It was completely pointless.

"Thank—you—so—much," Nina muttered as she fished around inside the car door with the ruler. She had managed to slide the metal strip between the window and the rubber strip things holding it in place, but that's as far as it went. "Thanks a million for your help, Charlie Hay-flippin'-ward!" She gave a few more half-hearted downward stabs with the ruler, then she gave up. "Those BCAA people obviously know something I don't. Should have taken that automechanics class in Grade 11, after all." She had signed up for it together with her boyfriend, but then he broke up with her, and she had dropped the class like a hot potato and taken Art Metal instead. She'd overheard him bragging about learning how to do this stuff, and she had turned up her nose at it. She didn't need any of that, she'd told herself, as there'd always be a knight in shining armour available to do it for her, or at any rate, a mechanic in shining tow truck, just a phone call away. She'd certainly not figured on being phone-less in the wilderness, and having the knight in shining lumberjacket go AWOL as soon as there was any real work to be done.

"Gah!" Nina tossed the ruler to the ground and leaned back against the hood of the car. Now what was she going to do?

Nina's phone rang, and she jumped. Automatically she clapped her hand to her jeans pockets—where had she put it, where was it? The ringing was kind of quiet, muffled; she couldn't feel the buzzing—wait. It was in the car, of course. D'uh. With a groan, Nina leaned her forehead against the driver's door window. There was her phone, in her purse on the passenger seat; she could see the whole bag vibrating from the buzzing. It rang, rang, rang—then stopped. Faintly, Nina could hear the plonk-plink noise of an incoming voicemail. And then the phone started ringing again. Ringing, ringing, shaking the bag—vibrating so much, it slid right out of the bag. It slipped off the seat and landed screen upmost on the floor of the car. "June Mauser," the display said in bright yellow letters, and Nina's boss' picture flashed on the screen.

Oh brother.

If June was this desperate to get a hold of Nina, there was some major crisis afoot. And June would be royally pissed that Nina wasn't answering. Locking yourself out of your car and being unable to get help to open the door was highly unlikely to count as a good reason with her. Nina had lived in the city all her life, but she was a downright country girl compared to June. June would never comprehend that out in the woods, there *was* no help to be gotten. Nina knew she would get zero understanding from her boss, let alone sympathy. June hadn't shown any understanding for Nina turning off her phone while she was at her neighbour's funeral; an inconvenient accident during a few days off would hardly rate a better reaction.

The ringing stopped for a few seconds, then started right up again.

Nina banged her head against the door of the car. Her job was already hanging by a thread; this might be the last straw.

What could she do? She needed to get into her car, needed to get in touch with June to find out what the woman wanted. It was quite possible that she was having a fit because she couldn't find one of the files they were working on—but maybe it was actually something really important this time, a crisis with one of their clients—something only Nina knew where to find... Or something stupid and trivial, like June having forgotten the name of her favourite nail polish. It wouldn't be the first time. But the dumb thing was, there was no telling until Nina actually *talked* to her.

There was no other option: Nina had to get to town. She wracked her brains to try to remember the image on Google Maps when she'd vaguely glanced at it. The town—Houghton, Charlie had called it?—had been, umm, down the street where she'd come from, then left, correct? She'd made a right off the street that was going to, eventually, lead to the town, so if she kept walking back the way she'd come and then turned left at the end of it, she should eventually get to the turnoff towards Houghton. A turnoff to the right, she thought.

Well, there was only one way to find out.

With a rueful glance at her feet in their strappy sandals Nina set off down the road.

She was deep in the woods out here, and she hadn't paid attention what was along the road when she was driving in, as she'd been focused on getting to the cottage, listening for Google Maps' "In. Five hundred metres. You have arrived at. Your destination." Some hundred metres or so past the hedge in front of the cottage was a narrow path going in between two bushes, but Nina didn't think it would lead anywhere she'd want to be. The road was her best bet.

The end of the road seemed a lot farther when you were on foot than it had appeared by car. By the time Nina reached the point where Hawthorn Lane joined the paved road, her sandal had already rubbed a sore spot on the baby toe of her left foot. Botheration. But there was nothing else to do—she had to keep going. She turned left and kept on trudging. The road was somewhat wider here than the street the cottage was on, a deep ditch on both sides, pines on either side. Typical BC Interior—miles and miles of miles and miles, trees and mountains all the way. Nina sighed. There wasn't a turn-off in sight. Nature and the great outdoors was all fine and dandy, but walking eight kilometres through the woods... she could think of more fun ways to spend a day.

Suddenly there came a wind blast, whipping her hair over her face. A cold wind blast. And it got dark, like someone had drawn a curtain across the sun. What the heck? Nina looked up. Where there had been clear blue sky before, the sky was covered in dark thunderclouds, roiling and tumbling over one another. Oh man—just what she needed!

Nina hesitated for a moment. Was there any chance she was actually closer to the town than to the cottage yet? It seemed she'd walked for a long time—but had it been that far yet?

Another wind blast hit her straight in the face, and a thick raindrop splashed on her arm.

"That does it!" Nina turned around. Getting back to the cottage was the thing to do. She couldn't exactly run in those sandals, but getting back sooner rather than later would probably be a good thing. It wasn't raining full-out yet, but it would be any minute now.

She was a couple hundred metres away from the cottage when the clouds burst for real and a deluge dumped on her head. She put on a burst of speed, half running, half limping, swearing at the way her feet squished in the wet sandals. The side of her toe was being rubbed raw by her sandal, and the cold rain plastered her hair down, pouring down her neck and into her T-shirt. She hunched her shoulders and ran for it, reached the gate in the hedge and shoved it open.

"Yuck!" she cried as the hedge dumped another load of water down her neck, "yuck, yuck, yuck, yuck!"

The garden was dripping and gurgling and murmuring as Nina jumped up the three steps to the porch. She dug in her pocket for the key and opened the door, took a step in and then back out again onto the porch. She shook herself like a dog and wrung out her hair, dripping like a wash cloth, then stepped back into the house, dim in the overcast afternoon.

A cold breeze came from the French doors.

"Oh good grief, I never closed them before I left!" There was a puddle on the floor in front of them, and the doormat seemed to have gotten wet, too. Nina sprinted down the short hallway and grabbed a towel from the bathroom, ran back into the living room, and threw the towel on the floor by the doors. She stood up, her eyes still on the towel on the floor, reached for the handles of the French doors—and screamed.

There stood Charlie, right outside the doors on the overgrown patio, dripping with rain, his head hunched between his shoulders, looking thoroughly bedraggled. He was clutching what looked like a bottle of wine in one hand and hiding something under his lumberjacket with the other, giving Nina a pathetic look, half smile, half helpless grimace.

"Ugh! You—you—" Nina had her hands in claws and shook them at him in her reaction to the fright. "Stop freaking me out like this! And don't bother apologizing if you keep doing it, I don't want to hear it!" She stepped back and made an impatient gesture. "Get your butt in here, I'm not leaving the door open!"

He heaved a sigh of relief and stepped into the room.

"Thanks," he said, shivering. He put the bottle of wine on the wood crate coffee table and fished the thing out from under his jacket. It turned out to be a round loaf of bread, with a couple of strange holes punched into the crust. "Brought a peace offering," he said with a sheepish smile. "I don't think it got too soggy in the rain."

"Why the heck didn't you just walk in?" Nina said with irritation. Being startled made her grumpy.

"Can't, not without an invitation," he said.

She looked up from where she was mopping up the rainwater puddle and gave him a frown.

"Seems kind of stupid," she said. "You can take politeness too far, you know. You could have closed the doors behind you while you were at it."

"Yeah, well. I'm sor—"

"Don't!" Nina said, holding up her hand. "*Don't* say you're sorry, I don't want to hear it." Her thumping heartbeat was settling down a little, and her temper with it.

Charlie took off his soaked lumberjacket. "Do you mind if I put this in the kitchen?" he said. "It did get rather damp." His curls were black with wetness, dripping water onto his shoulders, and the mac jacket had dark patches of moisture running down the back.

"Yeah, sure," she said, "it's over there." She pointed at the archway to the kitchen. "Do you need a towel to dry off?"

"Yes, that would be good," he said, turning his head away, not looking at her. "You might want to, uh, yourself..."

"What?" Nina looked down at herself and gave a little scream, clapping her arms across her chest. Her soaked T-shirt had gone completely transparent, and she was standing there in not much more than her bra. "Ugh, ugh,

ugh…" She ran down the hall to the bathroom, wrenched open the door, darted in and slammed it behind her. Did she hear a chuckle coming from the kitchen? That—that *man*!

A quarter hour later, she came back out into the living room, feeling self-conscious. She was wearing one of the blouses and a skirt she had found in the bedroom closet, with a pair of woolly socks and a knitted wool sweater over top. She'd had to roll up the sleeves on both the blouse and sweater a bit; otherwise everything fit really well. Even more important than the fit, though, they were dry. Her sopping wet jeans and T-shirt were hanging over the shower curtain rail to dry.

Charlie was kneeling in front of the fireplace, and he looked around as she entered.

"You look charming," he said with an eye-crinkling smile.

"Yeah, well, it's dry," Nina said. "And quite comfortable, actually. Thanks for the compliment. What are you doing?"

"Making a fire," he said, "if you don't mind."

"Oh! No, I—where did you find the wood?"

"There's still a wood pile beside the house," he said, splitting small pieces of wood off a larger one with a somewhat rusty-looking hatchet.

"You mean you went back out in that?" She gestured out the French doors at the pouring rain.

He shrugged. "Couldn't get much wetter," he said. His jeans were dark with water over his thighs, and Nina saw his work boots standing by the french doors; he had on a pair of grey woollen socks with a hole in the right toe. The T-shirt that was stretched over his broad shoulders was visibly damp, and the water that dripped from his hair made it even wetter than it was already.

"You never got that towel," Nina said. "There's a couple of dry ones in the bathroom, down that—"

"I know," he said, stacking his pieces of kindling in the middle of the fireplace.

He knew, did he? Hmph.

"Let me finish building this fire," he said, "then I'll take you up on that offer. I think we could both use some warmth." He carefully balanced some larger log pieces over top of the smaller kindling in the middle.

"Yes," Nina said. "Actually, how about some tea?"

He looked up from the wood. "I'd love a cup! Thank you." His British accent had become quite pronounced at that last statement. Nina shook her head. Who *was* this guy? She wandered into the kitchen, put the kettle on the stove and took out the tea tin.

"I've only got powdered milk," she said, sticking her head back into the living room.

"That's all right, I take it black."

He reached up on the mantelpiece, took down the box of matches, then opened a little cupboard door beside the fireplace, reached in and took out a newspaper. He pulled out one of the sheets and twisted it into a sausage shape, poking it into the middle of his stacked wood for a fire starter.

Nina hadn't even noticed that cupboard door before, let alone known that there was newspaper in there.

"All right, how come you know so much about this house?" she said, marching over to the fireplace and picking up the outer sheet of newspaper he had dropped there.

He shrugged. "It's kind of a long story."

But Nina only half heard him. She was staring at the paper. "What the heck—this is from 1998!" Weirdly enough, it wasn't yellowed at all.

"Like I said, long story."

Nina looked from Charlie to the paper and back again, then she shook her head and dropped the paper back on the hearthstone.

"Whatever!"

The kettle started the shriek of its whistle, and she went to the kitchen to make the tea.

When she came back into the living room with the two mugs full of piping hot black tea, Charlie was standing over the fire, his hands stretched out towards it, trying to warm himself. His head was tousled, but no longer dripping; apparently he had made use of the towels in the bathroom. Nina put the mugs on the coffee table and sat down on the couch.

"Why don't you stop looming and sit yourself down?" she said, picking up her mug and cradling it between her hands.

"Don't want to leave a water stain on the couch," he said, indicating his soaking wet jeans.

"Oh," said Nina, "fair enough." She didn't have any pants to offer him to change into, but—oh, wait! "Hey, wait a second," she said. She ran down the hall into the bedroom, pulled open the bottom dresser drawer, and took out a pair of the brown dungarees. "Look, these might..." she called, turning around—and she jumped again, finding him right behind her.

"Cut—it—out!!" she cried, actually smacking him in the chest this time.

He caught her wrist. "I'm—"

"No, you're not," she said irritably, wrenching free her wrist. "Or you'd stop doing this. Here,"—she shoved the dungarees at him—"they might fit you. Or not. But at least they're dry."

"Thanks," he said, backing up a step. "I really don't mean to startle you, honestly. I thought you heard me following you."

"Yeah, well, I didn't," Nina said, grumpy. "You'll need to stomp louder, I guess. Besides, you shouldn't follow a girl into her bedroom, anyway. If you know this house, then you knew that's where I was going."

He looked embarrassed. "Uh, sor—Umm, I mean, I'll, uh, you know..." He gestured with the pants in his hands and disappeared into the bathroom, locking the door behind him with a click.

Nina took a deep breath to calm herself down. Hmph!

By the time Charlie came out of the bathroom again Nina had had several long sips of her tea, and her toes were starting to feel toasty at the nice fire he'd started, so she felt more kindly disposed towards him.

When she caught sight of him the last bit of irritation vanished, and she burst out laughing. The pants were at least two inches too short on him, exposing the red stripe at the top of his woolly grey socks.

He looked down on himself and grinned. "Yeah, I guess Miran—" He broke off.

Nina gave him a look. "Miranda *what*? That's what you were going to say, 'I guess Miranda—', wasn't it?"

He twisted his mouth sideways in a rueful look, but didn't say anything.

"Okay, that's it," said Nina. "*Sit!*" She emphatically stabbed her finger at the couch cushion beside her. "And *talk*."

He obediently lowered himself onto the other end of the couch. Nina could smell his slightly musky scent, and his wet T-shirt gave off an odour of dampness.

"So, who is, or was, Miranda?"

Charlie picked up his mug, cupped his hands around it, inhaled the fragrance of the steam, then took a sip, closing his eyes in bliss, leaning his head against the back of the couch, savouring the tea.

Stalling techniques, all of them.

"Ah, lovely cuppa," he said after another sip. "I missed this..."

"Uh-huh," said Nina impatiently. "Quit putting me off. Who's Miranda?"

He shot her a glance out of the corner of his eye. "Well, it was worth a try," he said. "But it really is a lovely cup of tea, truly."

"And your English heart rejoices, I know. Now answer my question."

"It does!" he protested. "And how did you know I'm English?"

"You have an accent," Nina said curtly. "I collect accents. Answer. My. Question. Or I'll take away your cuppa and kick you out in the rain again."

"You wouldn't!" he said plaintively, hugging the mug to his chest.

Nina glared at him. "Try me."

He laughed and spread his hand upwards in a gesture of defeat. "All right then, cruel and merciless lady—whose name I still don't know... Won't you tell me what it is?"

Nina shot out her hand and snatched the mug from his fingers. "There—Ouch!" The hot tea splashed out over her hand and his. She nearly dropped the mug, but in an instant, Charlie had clapped both his hands around the outside of hers, catching the cup and her. There was a heartbeat of silence as his hands trapped hers around the warmth of the mug, and his blue eyes bored into hers, the expression on his face utterly serious.

Nina blinked and started breathing again.

"Nina," she said, "it's Nina."

His face relaxed into a smile, and he loosened his hold on her hands and the mug. "Thank you, Nina." He dug in the pocket of the dungarees and brought out a white square of cloth that he used to dry his fingers and then dab at the large wet patch on his thigh. "Seems like I'm doomed to wetness today. And please, lady, may I have my tea back?" He held out the cloth.

Nina let him take the mug from her hands. "You carry a handkerchief?" she said, wiping her hands with it. "That's kind of old-fashioned."

"A gentleman should never be without one, my mother always said. Good thing I transferred it from my jeans." He took a sip from his tea, but he had to tip the mug rather far to get some out of it. "Not much left," he said. "Please, ma'am, may I have some more?"

Nina raised her eyebrows. "Fine, seeing as I was the one who spilled it on you. But don't think it's getting you out of answering my question." She rose and got the teapot from the kitchen.

He held out his mug. "Which question was that then?"

Nina pulled back the teapot, from which she had been about to pour, and gave him a look.

He laughed. "All right, all right, I'll talk, but *please* let me have more tea!"

Even so, he took a long sip before he began talking, and then his eyes were on the crackling flames in the fireplace.

"Miranda," he said slowly. "Miranda McManus. She—well, this was her house."

"Yes, I know," Nina said a little impatiently. "But who *was* she?"

"She was my friend," he said, still in that slow voice, gazing at the fire. "Without her, I wouldn't be here."

"What, you mean 'here' here, as in this house, or you wouldn't 'be here', like, exist?"

"Well... I came over from England and started a handyman's business—repair work, landscaping, whatever people wanted. Miranda hired me to help her with the garden, and we became good friends. She was—special."

"What was she like?"

"You mean to look at? Smallish. A bit taller than you, but not much. Red hair—or it once was; by the time I knew her it was mostly grey. Just a nice, older lady. Those were hers." He gestured at the clothes Nina was wearing and the pair of overalls he had on.

"I figured," Nina said. "It's kind of weird wearing the clothes of someone who you've never even met. And even weirder if they fit."

"I'll bet."

"So, why would she leave me her property? I never even heard of her before. What was she doing—I mean, did she have a job or something?"

"She lived on her own—probably had investments or such. As for why she chose you, I couldn't say. Perhaps she knew your parents?"

Nina raised her eyebrows. "You know, that's a possibility," she said. "I'll have to give my mom a call—shoot, my phone is in my car." She ran her hands through her hair. Charlie gave her a look, and Nina felt self-conscious. She wasn't trying to flirt by fiddling with her hair—was she? "So, you don't know anything about why she made her will the way she did—leaving everything to me, I mean."

"To you in particular, no. I don't recall her ever mentioning a Nina. Is that your Christian name?"

"My given name, you mean?" Nina made a face. "Uh, no."

He gave her a sideways glance. "No?"

"No."

"So? What is it then?"

Nina squirmed. But if it would help figure out this mystery... "It's Virginia, if you must know. Virginia Marie Takahashi, the full thing. Don't you dare laugh!"

"I'm not," he said with a perfectly straight face. "What's wrong with that name?"

"It sounds like someone's maiden aunt!"

"Well, *are* you someone's maiden aunt?"

She gave him a dirty look. "That's not the point! And for your information, no, I'm not."

"Maiden or aunt? No, please don't hit me!" He ducked, crooking his arm over his head.

"Hmph!" Nina put down her hand again. "Anyway, it sounds like someone who wears cardigans and carries peppermints in her purse. I've never liked it."

"Virginia is not a bad name," he said. "You know, Virginia Woolf and all that. And you *are* wearing a cardigan at the moment."

Nina looked down at herself. "Yeah, but it's not mine. And I've never felt like a Virginia. Plus, the teasing..."

Charlie had a sympathetic look on his face. "I can see that," he said. "So you went by Nina then?"

"Yes, since Grade 9. Who's Virginia Woolf?"

He raised his eyebrows. "You don't know Virginia Woolf?"

"The name sounds familiar, but I can't place it a the moment. 'Who's afraid of Virginia Woolf' rings a bell, though."

"That's a stage play—it hasn't really got much to do with her," Charlie said. "Woolf was a writer—English, 1920s, Bloomsbury Group? No?"

Nina shook her head.

"Oh, wait a moment," he said standing up from the couch. "I think—wasn't there..."

He walked down the hall, went into the bedroom, and came back with a book in his hand.

"See, I knew it. A copy of *Orlando.*" He handed the book to Nina.

"Oh, that one! I didn't realize that was Virginia what's-her-name. Wasn't there a movie made of it? It had Tilda Swinton in it. Some kind of cross-gender story."

Charlie wrinkled his forehead, then it cleared again. "Oh yes, I remember seeing that in the theatre."

"Really? I thought it was quite old, like, from the early 90s." He would have had to have been a little kid at the time, and this was hardly a children's story.

"Oh, umm, yeah." Charlie looked away from her, down at the fire again. "So you haven't read the book?" He put his feet up on the wood crate coffee table and leaned back against the sofa cushions.

"Can't say I have. But hey, how come you knew there was a copy in the bedroom?"

He wiggled the toe that stuck up out of the hole in his sock. "I told you, I was Miranda's handyman. I fixed things in this house."

"I thought you said you worked in her garden."

"Yes, that, too. So if you haven't read Virginia Woolf, what do you read? *Do* you read?"

She looked at him with her eyebrows raised. "Oh, no, I don't read, I only go on Netflix binges. Sheesh!"

"What-flix binges?"

"Oh-kay... You don't know what Netflix is? Streaming video, movies over the Internet?"

"Oh, the Internet, yes, of course." That sounded like he didn't actually know what was going on. He didn't have a cell phone, but did he not even have a computer?

"Uh—don't you get cable out here—wifi, that sort of thing?"

"Is there any more tea?" He was obviously trying to change the subject. That was just weird.

Nina hoisted the teapot and swirled it. "The smallest of dribbles." She poured it into his mug. "Do you want me to make some more?"

"That would be fantastic," he said. "Yes, please! And we could slice this up and make toast." He picked up the loaf of bread he'd brought.

"I don't have a toaster. Or power to run it, even if there was one in the kitchen."

"Who needs a toaster when there's a fire?"

"Oh, like toasting marshmallows? I guess that could work," Nina said, walking into the kitchen with the teapot. She turned on the tap and filled the kettle. "And there's jam," she called out over the sound of the running water. "No butter, though. Do you have any at your house we could use?"

There was no response from the living room. Nina put the kettle on the burner and turned up the flame.

"Hey, Charlie, I said, do you have any butter at your house? Or margarine, that would do too."

Still no answer. Nina walked back into the living room and did a double-take.

"Where did you go? Charlie?" His spot on the couch was empty. Was he back in the bedroom, checking out her—or rather, Miranda's—bookshelf again? But he'd left the *Orlando* book sitting on the coffee table. Nina walked down the hall and stuck her head into the bedroom. Not there. Oh, of course, he had probably gone to the bathroom, the door was closed.

"Hey, you in there?" Nina knocked on the bathroom door. But it wasn't actually closed—it slowly creaked open.

"Uh, Charlie?"

Silence.

Nina pushed the bathroom door all the way open. It was as empty as the bedroom. What the heck? Charlie's wet jeans were draped over the shower curtain rod next to Nina's pants and her T-shirt. But no sign of the guy himself. Where'd he got to? Run out wearing Miranda's too-short overalls? She hadn't heard the door open or close—but then, the sound of the running water had been kind of loud. But why would he leave without saying anything, and without his own jeans? And his mac jacket was still in the kitchen, too.

Nina shook her head and wandered back into the living room. The loaf of bread was sitting on the coffee table crate, next to the book and Charlie's empty mug. Nina could hear the kettle in the kitchen, just coming to a boil again and starting its shrill whistle.

She didn't actually feel like having another cup of tea herself—she'd only put on the kettle for Charlie. With a slight "so there" feeling, she hoisted it off the burner and turned off the gas. If the guy wasn't sticking around for the tea he'd asked for, that was his problem. You snooze, you lose.

Maybe she'd give that *Orlando* book a try—it was still pouring rain outside, no point in going out again. And maybe she should ask Charlie for proper directions before trying it again, anyway. If the guy ever showed up again.

Bear

The rain had emptied itself out in the night, and there was a brilliantly blue sky visible between the tree tops when Nina got out of bed in the morning. She pushed aside Charlie's jeans on the shower rod—they were still slightly damp—and thoughtfully looked at the tub. She'd love a bath, but there was no hot water. A cold dip didn't seem appealing. Also, there was no shampoo. But at least there was soap to wash the rest of her—and hopefully she'd get into her car today, so she'd have her toiletries again. She shuffled into the kitchen and put on the kettle for some warm water to have a sponge bath.

So, what to do today? A bowl of oatmeal for breakfast would be good, maybe with some strawberries from the garden. And then another attempt to get to town. With this weather, at least she wouldn't have to turn around on account of rain.

She found a pair of hiking boots in the bottom of the closet in the bedroom, which, like the clothes, were exactly her size. She put on her jeans, which had dried overnight. So had the T-shirt, but it needed a wash. What about those blouses in the closet? There were certainly enough of them, nice ones that actually wouldn't look too bad with jeans and hiking boots.

She picked one that was a lovely clear soft blue—kind of like Charlie's eyes, she found herself thinking, then she quickly shook off the thought. And told herself off for having her gaze stray to the French doors repeatedly, wondering if he would be standing outside, looking sheepish or apologetic for taking off without saying anything. He certainly didn't seem shy about apologizing, which was worth something in a guy. Or a girl, for that matter. If June would admit once in a while she'd been wrong, she wouldn't be so horrible to work for. Which made Nina think of the irate voicemail—or voicemails, rather, as there were bound to be a whole slew of them by now—that were waiting for her if or when she finally got into her car to answer her phone.

She *had* to get some help... Charlie was less than reliable, and apparently he wasn't making an appearance this morning. So with a sigh, Nina set out down the road, in the direction she figured town would be. She passed the little path leading between the bushes off the road—and stopped dead, smacking herself in the forehead with the flat of her hand. There was a house number sign there! She hadn't even seen that last time. A wooden sign with the number "2545" engraved on it drunkenly leaned against a tree trunk. So there was a house there!

They were bound to have a phone.

Unless that place stood empty too. With a dubious glance at the dilapidated sign, Nina turned down the driveway. There were trees quite close to the road, and the wheelruts seemed rather overgrown. She began to have doubts. Maybe all the houses around here were abandoned? This yard didn't seem a whole lot better taken care of than that of her own house—her *own* house, which was a weird thought. The main difference was that this property was all forested and had apparently never had a well-planted garden like hers.

Well, there was the house, visible through the trees. Pink siding, tall windows, fake shutters, gingerbread trim. Nina couldn't see any cars in front, but maybe they had a garage out back or something.

She turned along the S-curve of the driveway and walked around a boulder, heading for the front door of the house.

A huge black shape reared up in front of her.

A bear!

It stood at least six feet high, staring at Nina from its small eyes, its big black paws dangling in front of its chest.

Ice-cold panic rushed through Nina, and for a moment she felt completely paralyzed. Her heart skipped a beat, then it began racing, a massive clanging noise sounding in her ears as she stared at the animal. It was clacking its teeth and huffing at her.

Her legs shaking so badly she could hardly stay upright, Nina slowly backed away—one tiny step at a time, her breath coming in gasps.

The bear stood there, staring at her, then it gave one more huff, dropped down on all fours and lumbered away in the other direction.

Nina kept backing up, slowly, slowly—she watched the bear disappearing around the back side of the house, then she turned and ran for her life, sobbing with fright. She raced along the driveway of the house—was that the sound of the bear thumping after her through the underbrush?—down the street, and then she crashed through the gate in the hedge and into her own garden. A long thick vine snagged her foot, and she stumbled forward.

She collided with a body. For an instant, she thought she felt rough fur, smelled an animal's harsh scent, and her heart seemed to stop, a loud whimper escaping her.

But no—these were human arms wrapping around her, muscular and firm.

"Whoa, what's the matter?" Charlie's voice asked.

Nina's breath came in sobbing gasps.

"It—it—there's—it's—a bear!" She could barely get the words out between sobs, and she frantically gestured behind her. "It—there—coming—need to get—inside!" Her knees buckled.

"Come on." He had his arm around her and half carried, half pushed her to the porch steps.

Nina stumbled up the stairs and fumbled the key out of her pocket. Her fingers shook so badly she barely got it into the lock, but then she was inside the door.

Charlie still stood at the bottom of the porch steps.

"Quick, get in, shut the door!" she cried frantically, tugging on the key to get it out of the lock.

He leapt up onto the porch, took the key from her hand, stepped inside, and firmly closed and locked the door behind them.

"Come here," he said, pulling Nina into his arms. "It's all right now, it's okay!" He wrapped his arms tightly around her and held her close. "It's all right, darling. He's gone, the bear is gone. You're safe, he's not going to hurt you. It's all right." He hugged her head to his chest.

Nina's sobs grew quieter.

"It's all right now," he said again, rubbing his hand over her back. "That was a bad fright, wasn't it, darling?"

She drew a shuddering breath. "I—I—" she sniffled into the soft fabric of his black T-shirt.

He let go of her head. "You're all right now, darling." He tucked a strand of her hair behind her ear. "You're okay."

Nina leaned her forehead against his broad chest. She could feel the beating of his heart under his firm chest muscles, and his arms were warm and comforting. She wrapped her arms around his waist and held on, closing her eyes and breathing in his musky scent; she could feel her racing heart slowing down and returning to its normal pace.

Oh, but—she became aware that her cheek was getting an imprint of the button that held up the straps of the brown overalls. He was still wearing those? And where did he get off calling her "darling"—even in that cute English accent of his?

She let go of his waist and leaned back to get out of his arms. He let go.

"Yeah," she said, "well..." She sniffled, running the back of her hand under her nose. "I—I—"

Charlie smiled down at her, then dug his hand into his pocket and brought out his handkerchief. She took it, embarrassed, and wiped her nose, taking perhaps a bit longer than usual, to hide her face for a minute.

"That—that was the—the scariest thing I—I ever ex—experienced," she said, when she couldn't draw out the nose-wiping any longer.

"I'll bet." He put his hand on her back and guided her to the couch. "Sit down, you're still shaking."

"I su-suppose that was a stupid thing, running from a bear," she said. She had heard bear safety rules before, and "don't run" was one of them. "But, I c—couldn't think straight. And he—he went the other way, behind that house. I j—just wanted to get away from there."

"I can understand that," Charlie said.

He was perched on the arm of the sofa, his hand on Nina's shoulder, rubbing it reassuringly. It felt so comforting that it took Nina a minute to realize what he was doing. She twitched her shoulder a bit, and he immediately took his hand off. Nina almost felt sorry for it.

"I'll make you a cup of tea," he said. "You need something warm and sweet." He got up from the couch arm.

"Okay," Nina said, looking up at him. Her eye fell on the brown overalls, far too short for him, and a slightly hysterical giggle made its way up her throat. "You forgot your jeans here yesterday," she said.

He looked down at his exposed ankles. "Yes, I know," he said. "I was hoping I could get them back. Wearing floods really isn't all it's cracked up to be."

"Don't you own any other pants?" Nina asked. "By the way, that's not your house, the one with the b—bear, is it?"

"What? No, oh no. Not my house. Definitely not." He gave a slight shudder. "Do you take milk in your tea?" he asked over his shoulder as he walked into the kitchen.

"Milk powder is all there is," Nina said. "But yes, please."

When he came back with a mug of tea for Nina, it turned out he had not only put milk in it, but about three spoons of sugar. Nina made a face. "That's—sweet," she said.

"You've had a shock; sugar helps," he said, taking a sip from his own tea and settling down at the other end of the couch.

"Well then... I can use all the help I can get." Nina lifted the mug for another sip, but found her hands were still shaking rather badly. She put the mug back on the coffee table. "I don't think I'll get over this in a hurry."

"Quite." He put his feet in their too-short pants up on the table, his toe sticking up through the hole in the sock. Still the same pair of socks, too?

Nina snickered.

"Your jeans are in the bathroom," she said. "I think they're dry."

He pulled on his pant legs to hitch them up a little more, exposing hairy shins. "Are you saying that I'm not the height of fashion in this outfit? I'm deeply wounded—I'm aiming to set a new trend here, you know." He wiggled his toe. "Hayward's Hayricks—rustic fashions for any eventuality, air holes included. For the discerning country gentleman or gentlewoman."

Nina laughed. "Thank you, I'll pass. I don't think it's quite my style. And I don't have the hairy legs to pull it off. Besides, I've kind of had enough of fur for the mo—" Her voice hitched as the fright came flooding back, wiping the laughter from her face.

"Now, now, now. None of that," Charlie said in a mock-stern voice. "No more crying. Not when I successfully locked the beast outside to protect you. I want to see a smile." He tipped his head down and sideways to look at her face. "Go along, smile for me!"

Nina blinked to hold back tears.

"No, no," he said. "Come on, laugh." He put his arm around Nina and tickled her in the ribs.

She squealed and jumped, her arm flying out in a reflex and knocking into his other hand that was still holding his tea cup. With a gush, the tea emptied over his lap. Now she did laugh outright.

"There, that served you right," she said.

He gave a rueful chuckle. "I suppose so," he said. "It was all intentional, of course, in the service of a lady in distress. You have to admit, I did make you laugh."

"You're weird," she said, bumping her arm against his side. "But, hey—thanks for cheering me up."

He tightened his arm around her. "You're very welcome," he said. "I'm sorry you got so scared."

Nina leaned against Charlie, sucked in a deep breath and let it back out again, blowing away the last of the fear. "Yeah, well, me too," she said. His arm was very comfortable to lean into... She looked down at the big wet patch on his crotch. "You might want to go get changed."

"Yes, I suppose." He made no move to take his arm away from around her.

"That has to be uncomfortable," Nina said. "Or are you getting so used to getting soaked that it doesn't matter anymore?"

"Something like that. But you're right, it doesn't feel great to have the sensation of having peed your pants. Haven't done that since I was six, on my second day of Year 2 of primary school. Worst day of my life—well, it was, until..."

"Until what?"

He disengaged his arm and hoisted himself off the couch. "I have to get these trousers changed."

Nina gave him a look as he stalked down the hall, his legs spread. This thing of ignoring her questions was getting a little irritating.

"So does that bear live around here?" she asked when he re-emerged from the bathroom, wearing his jeans. "Is it going to jump on me every time I set foot outside the house?"

"Uh, well..." He scratched his head.

"Because if it does," Nina continued, "I'm not going outside anymore!"

"Oh, no. Don't worry about that. He—he wouldn't hurt anyone."

Nina scoffed. "Could have fooled me!" she said. "He *roared* at me! That..."

"No, he didn't."

"What do you mean? Of course he did!"

"Black bears don't roar. It's more of a huffing."

"Hah, you weren't there! But fine then, he *huffed* at me! That was the freakiest thing in my entire life! Who's to say he wouldn't have eaten me next?"

"I say. He wouldn't," Charlie said as if he knew what he was talking about. "But really—"

"How the heck do you know?" Nina was starting to sound a bit hysterical, even to her own ears.

"—but really," he continued, talking over her, "I'd stay away from that house, if I were you. Not because of the bear, but—"

"But what? The bear is enough for me, thank you very much. What's worse than a bear? A serial rapist who sits in there like a spider in a web?"

"No, no, not that," he said, "but please, stay away from there." His face was so serious Nina's sarcastic reply dried up on her tongue.

"All I wanted was to ask if I could use their phone," she said. "I have to get out of here!"

In an instant, Charlie's face changed, and he grinned at her.

"Why? Is my company so irksome that you can't bear to stay here for a little while longer?"

"Bear—haha." Nina grimaced.

"Sorry, didn't mean that." Charlie held out his hand to her. "Come on," he said, "to prove to you there's no vicious ursine out there, let's go outside and pick some raspberries. That bear never comes into this garden—ever."

Nina let him pull her to her feet.

"How do you know? I thought bears liked berries."

"They do, but this particular one—well, let's just say Miranda made sure the garden is—protected."

"I didn't see a bear fence anywhere—unless that's what that thorny hedge out front is all about?"

Charlie was still holding Nina's hand, and he pulled open the French doors as he was talking. "That hedge is a hawthorn, and no, not particularly planted for the bear. But it keeps out ... others." He stepped out onto the patio, pulling Nina with him.

Nina still felt jumpy. "There! Are you sure that wasn't a bear? That sounded like something walking around out there!"

"Yes, I'm sure," he said. "Absolutely sure, darling."

"I'm not your darling!" Nina said, pulling her hand out of his.

"Certainly you are," he said casually, picking a few of the shiny black berries off the bushes that covered the patio.

Nina got distracted. "What are those? You can't just eat any old thing you find growing there! Aren't those deadly nightshade?"

Charlie laughed. "Not even close," he said. "They are perfectly harmless and perfectly delicious black currants." He picked a few more and held them out on the flat of his hand to Nina. "Try some! Come on, you know you want to."

"Do not!" said Nina. He was a little too sure of himself. But she took a couple of berries from his hand anyway, and gingerly put one in her mouth. "Hmm! This *is* black currant!" She recognized the flavour from her favourite Murchie's Tea variety.

"What, did you think I was lying?" He popped another handful of berries into his mouth. "Best jelly, black currant. There's red ones too, further back in the garden, but their season is already past."

"Oh, are they really small too? And kind of shrivelled now?"

"Yes, those are the ones." He was bending aside the bushes by the steps, holding back their branches.

"So what else is there in the garden?" Nina squeezed past him, purposely ignoring his nearness.

He let the bushes snap together behind her.

"Well, there are strawberries, raspberries, currants—black and red, blackberries, and I think there might still be a gooseberry bush beside the shed, but last time I saw it it wasn't doing very well."

"Last time you saw it?"

He ignored her again. "There are of course fruit trees—apples, pears, cherries, prune plums, greengages—"

"What the heck are those?"

"Oh, I guess they're not called that here. Miranda called them something else too. *Reine-claude*? No, that's the French name. It's a greenish-yellow soft plum, about so big." He made a small circle with his forefinger and thumb. "Nice bottled."

"Bottled? Oh, you mean canned." Nina skirted around a tall weedy bush.

"Yes, that." Charlie squeezed between the corner of the house and a tree trunk and pointed upwards. "See, there's the tree. Really needs pruning."

"Prune-ing, haha," Nina said. "I thought you said they were green-whatever plums, not prunes."

He grinned at her. "Greengages. And look, there are the raspberries."

The spiky hawthorn hedge seemed to go all the way around the garden. It bristled at Nina from beside the house. This was the right side of the house; the outside of the fireplace and chimney were rising in red brick up beyond the roof line. Between the house and the hedge was a thick tangle of vines. It was overgrown, with long tendrils snaking outwards, its bright green serrated leaves framing dense clusters of juicy scarlet fruits sparkling in the sunshine.

Nina could not suppress an exclamation of pleasure. "Those look so good!" she said.

"They *are* good," Charlie said, leaning over the tangle and pulling a berry off the vine. "Try?" He held it out to Nina.

She had no qualms whatever about those; raspberries she knew. And these ones were fantastic—huge, juicy, sweet, and fabulously flavourful. "Oh yum! We should have brought a bowl to put them in."

"Yes, indeed, we should have." Charlie was picking, alternately collecting the berries into his cupped hand and popping them into his mouth. "This is a thornless variety," he said around a mouthful of berries. "I'm glad I convinced Miranda to plant those rather than the regular kind."

"*You* convinced her?" Nina's fingers were stained bright red from the berries. Her hand was full of fruit, with no room left, so she ate whatever else she picked.

"Uh, yes. I helped her plant this garden."

Nine slewed her head around and looked at him. The garden had to be old—these raspberry bushes were totally overgrown. Nina didn't know how long berry bushes took to grow this tall and big, but certainly it would be more than a year or two. And Charlie—he looked not much more than thirty. Not enough time to have been there for the planting of this garden and still be around now. What was the deal?

Charlie pushed his way past her, raising the hand with the raspberries in them high over her head to fit past. "Let's put these in the kitchen," he said, "and we'll look if there are any strawberries left."

Nina followed him back through the bushes. "Strawberries which you also convinced Miranda to plant?" she asked skeptically.

Her doubtful tone seemed lost on Charlie. "No, not really," he said, squeezing through the black currant bushes, holding back the branches for Nina with his raspberry-free hand. "She knew what she wanted when it came to strawberries. They're everbearings, so you should get fruit off them all summer."

"All summer? That would require actually *being* here all summer."

His head flew around. "Won't you be?"

"Well…" No. Nina wasn't going to stay. The whole purpose of coming out here had been to check out this cottage, see what it was like, and then possibly find the nearest real estate agent and put the thing on the market. Someone was bound to want a nice little cottage in the woods for a holiday house, weren't they? And it wasn't like Nina had any use for it.

Except that now, for some reason, Nina felt curiously reluctant to say so. There was something about the cottage—no, not about Charlie, it didn't have anything to do with him. Oh no. It was the cottage itself, and the garden, that seemed to exert a strange pull on Nina, as if they wanted her to stay. As did Charlie, apparently.

Nina cleared her throat, pulled a cereal bowl out of the cupboard and spilled the raspberries from her hand into it. "So, strawberries?" She held the bowl out to Charlie, and he emptied his hand into it as well.

"Out back," he said, his hands under the kitchen tap, rinsing off the raspberry juice. "Let's bring a bowl this time."

Nina looked down on herself. "Oh, brilliant, I've got raspberry stains all over my pants. Do they come out?" Charlie shrugged, and Nina noticed that his jeans weren't in much better shape than hers. She huffed. "Hmph, who am I asking here?"

"It's the country, nobody cares," Charlie said. He reached into an upper cupboard and brought down a plastic bowl. "Here, I don't know if there are enough strawberries, but better safe than sorry, eh?"

There weren't, in fact, a lot of ripe strawberries—they ended up eating them right out there in the garden. But their bowl filled up anyway with a couple of small heads of the ruffled green lettuce, and several handfuls of both purple and green beans.

"Hmm, I wonder," Charlie said, wading through some thick greenery. "Let's see—hmm—they should be right about—Yes, here they are!" He put down the bowl, then pulled something off a few tangled and half-buried vines and held it out to Nina.

"Oh, peas!" Nina took one of the plump bright green pods on his palm.

"They used to be excellent," he said, pulling apart a pod and shelling out the little green balls with his thumb onto his palm. "Might not be the best anymore—it's a little past their season." He popped the peas in his mouth. "Ah, yes, not as tender as they would have been a few weeks ago."

Nina followed suit. The peas were a bit tough, but tasty.

"Let's take some of those too," she said, trying to get past Charlie to reach the pea vines. He didn't move out of the way, so she had to squeeze right up to him, and when she gave him a dirty look he just grinned at her.

"Got a problem, darling?" He waggled his eyebrows.

"Hmph!" Nina put her hands on his chest and shoved. "I am *not* your darling!"

He tried to step back to catch himself, but all that was behind him was a great tangle of bean vines, waist-high grass, red currant bushes, and downward-hanging apple tree branches. He overbalanced and fell backwards, half hanging in the tree branches.

"So there!" Nina said, then burst out laughing at the astonished look on his face. She reached out her hands to help him to his feet. "That'll larn you," she drawled, and she gave a great heave, pulling on his hands.

He grunted as she got him half-way up, and tried to find his balance. "It will indeed—darling." He grinned.

Nina let go, and with a yelp he dropped back into the bushes.

She crossed her arms, glaring at him sprawled in the vegetation at her feet, an apple twig poking into his ear. "You don't learn, do you?"

"I do, I do—eventually," he said and held out his hands. "Please, dear, kind Nina, help me up?"

"Hah, that's more like it!" Nina grabbed his hands and pulled—he was no lightweight, for sure. "Oof!"

He came all the way to his feet, but the inertia of her pull kept them going, and he tipped forward towards her. For a second, they stood pressed together, chest to chest, his face mere inches from hers, their hands clasped between them. Nina inhaled his spicy scent, his breath warm on her face; she could feel his heartbeat through his T-shirt. Her breath caught, and she stared up into his blue eyes. He gazed back at her, and his face got closer to hers, even closer...

Nina gave a small gasp and moved back, pulling her hands out of his grasp.

Charlie straightened up, his breath uneven.

"Peas!" Nina said, her voice a little unsteady, and she stepped past him.

She could hear him clear his throat behind her, then a rustle as if he was stepping back, but she concentrated hard on the tangled plants in front of her. Yes, there were the pea vines, and—ah yes, here, that was a pea pod. And another one here, and here.

“Pass me the bowl,” she said without turning around, holding out her hand behind her.

Nothing happened.

“Uh, Charlie, the bowl?” She wiggled the fingers of her outstretched hand.

Still nothing.

“Charlie, what—" She turned around.

He was gone.

Mad at Charlie

Gone again, out of the blue, without warning and without saying anything. It was too darn weird.

Nina refused to think about this any more. She would not. She was going around in circles in her head anyway, so she would just stop.

What was with the guy? What was going on? One minute he was there, the next he was gone. There was something not right about this—there really wasn't.

Oh, yes, she wasn't going to think about it, was she?

Because it wasn't right. It was weird, that's what it was—as weird as her getting the inheritance of this cottage in the first place, from a person she'd never heard of before—actually, quite a bit more so.

Nina gave a yank at a clump of grass. If it was grass. Charlie would probably tell her it was edible, and...

Not. Think. About. It.

Or him.

She ripped up another clump of grass, edible or not, and shook the dirt off the roots, then tossed it aside. There, at least that gave the strawberry plants a little bit of room to breathe. If they needed breathing; Nina had no idea. Charlie would probably—No!

She—was—not—thinking—about—the—man.

Nina levered herself to her feet and dusted her dirt-covered hands on the seat of her jeans. The pants were so filthy now, it probably didn't make no-never-mind, as Granny used to say.

Her eye fell on the shed door. Hmm. That metal ruler thing Charlie—ugh, him again! Nina put his name sternly out of her mind. The metal ruler thing *they had found* in that shed hadn't really helped much, but perhaps there was something else in there that could be useful? She *had* to get into her car, *had* to get out of this godforsaken place. And in spite of Cha—In spite of *having been reassured* that the bear wasn't usually around, Nina was not going out on the road on foot anymore.

She wiggled and yanked on the door handle, hard. It popped open so abruptly she stumbled back. The interior of the shed was still dark, dank and a bit scary. Nina wished Charlie—No, she did not wish that. Because she wasn't thinking about him, that's why. She could handle this on her own.

Taking a deep breath for courage, she took a step inside the shed. There was that rag, the one they had used before. Hmm, probably no point in checking the drawers of the work bench, they'd done that last time. Nina squatted down and started poking around under the work bench.

Ten minutes later, she emerged from the shed triumphant. A wire coat hanger—she had found a *wire coat hanger*! Not only that, she had managed to snip the thing off and bend it to shape with one of the rusty pairs of pliers that hung on the back of the work bench, and she was now brandishing a very rusty but decidedly curved wire hook.

"Car lock, here I come!" Nina said. She didn't need a man to rescue her, no way. Self-rescuing princess, that was her.

And sure enough, it took no time at all to push the coat hanger under the window seal and down into the door, and wiggle it back and forth until it caught on something. And—*click!*—the door lock knob came up!

Yes!! Nina almost sobbed out loud with relief. She had done it! She had fixed her problem, unlocked her car! She wiggled the coat hanger back out of the door, tossed it aside, and yanked up the door handle; the click of the opening door latch disengaging was sheer music to her ears. She pulled open the door, lunged across the driver's seat, snatched the keys from the ignition and shoved them into her jeans pocket. She was not going to let go of those keys again for a long, long time. Or her phone, for that matter. Nina plopped herself onto the driver's seat and leaned over, fishing for her phone on the floor of the passenger's side.

"Here, phonie phonie phone, here!" Her groping fingers met the smooth flat surface of the phone, and she picked it up. "Am I ever glad to see you!" she said, kissing the screen. "Nothing like being locked in a cottage without power or wifi to make you appreciate a good ol' cell phone!"

She pushed the "on" button, and the screen came to life. But instead of the picture of the West Coast beach that Nina had as her wallpaper, what met her eye was, prominently in the middle of the screen, a large symbol of a battery, only the bottom quarter of it still coloured in—in red. Then the screen went dark again.

"No! Oh come on, really? Dead battery?"

Nina started digging in her purse. She should be able to charge the phone from the cigarette lighter, right? But where was the charge cable? One longish, whitish cable, usually rolled up into a circle and stuffed somewhere... in the purse... right? She dug and rummaged. No no no—this couldn't be happening! Where was the cable? Nina upended the purse on the passenger seat, stuff spilling off the sides. Lipstick. Wallet. Apartment key. Comb. Small tube of hand cream. Compact with mirror. Packet of Kleenex. Another lipstick, two tubes of chapstick. One small box of Vicks throat candies, cherry flavour. Two envelopes containing bills—one hydro, one gas company. A miniature flashlight. One small pink can of dog spray. Really? She had dog spray in her purse? That was supposed to have been for defending herself from muggers and rapists on the streets of Downtown Vancouver, and she had completely forgotten that she had it in her purse. Hah, that might come in handy if Mr. Bear ever showed his face around her again! However, still no charge cable for the phone. One little USB-C cable, that was all she needed! Please please please...

Wait—had she put it in the glove compartment?

She whipped open the little flap in front of the passenger seat. Okay, sketch book. Car papers. Tiny travel watercolour box, Cotman brand. Small dropper bottle with water for moistening the watercolour cakes—originally the bottle had held liquid Tylenol. More paper tissues. A plastic bottle of drinking water. A pair of—believe it or not—gloves; what were those doing in the glove box? About a dozen crumpled up receipts from gas stations. One unpaid parking ticket for going over time in the parking lot off Carrall Street in Chinatown on her last dim sum trip. A bag of black tea candies bought on that same trip at the tea shop on East Pender and Columbia. Two red plastic Dairy Queen ice cream spoons (one short for Sundaes, one long for blizzards), one wooden soup spoon from a Tim Horton's chili, one small fork from Wendy's tossed salad. Paper napkins to match, as well as three packets of salt, two of pepper, and one scary-looking ketchup. Had she really bought fast food this often lately?

By the time Nina got this far, she didn't need to dig down to the bottom of the glove compartment to the half dozen mostly-dead ballpoint pens that resided in the far back to realize that, no, her phone charging cable wasn't there either.

Bother. Bother bother bother bother.

Well, at least she was no longer without transportation. She could go to that town, whatever its name was—Houghton, that was it—and pick up a spare cable. Even a little hick town in Backwoods Nowheresville should have a gas station, and most of those sold phone charge cables these days.

However, being out of power meant no internet and no Google Maps. That figured. Nina vowed to herself that in future, she'd never go anywhere out in the country again without buying a good old-fashioned paper map first. Not only had she lost the use of her phone for as long as she had (and now even longer), but it was anyone's guess whether there would be cell reception in this place. As it was, she had two options: get in the car and start driving, or... No, she didn't really have another option. Because she refused to think about Char—think about other options, that's why.

Ah well. First of all, she had to go to the bathroom. And she was not leaving that car without her stuff in tow. Once burned, twice shy—or as it were, once locked out, twice paranoid.

She stuffed all the clutter back into her purse and the glove compartment and hoisted her luggage out of the back seat of the car. It took some effort to pull her little suitcase across the road, its wheels rattling over the gravel. It wasn't exactly designed for the backwoods country; airport terminals were more what the designers had had in mind. As for the flagstones that led from the garden gate to the house—fortunately, the suitcase had handles. Nina's purse kept slipping off her shoulder as she hauled the luggage through the garden tangle and up onto the porch.

"Need a hand?" came Charlie's voice from behind her.

Nina jumped. Then she clenched her teeth, slowly put the suitcase down, and even more slowly turned around.

She pasted on her most charming smile. "Oh hi!" she said in a voice so sweet it almost brought on a toothache. "Fancy meeting you here! I would never have expected this; how fabulous to see you! How've you been? It's been *ages*!"

He looked startled. "Has it?"

Nina rolled her eyes. She could have done without the "stupid and innocent" act. Except, said a niggling little voice in the back of her mind, he seemed genuinely surprised... So she threw him a crumb. "Yeah, it's been all of, like, an hour. I could hardly bear it."

"Oh," he said. He hung his head and looked down at the toes of his thick work boots. "You're mad at me."

"Oh, no, really, am I?" Nina said, letting sarcasm drip from every word. "I had no idea. And whyever should I be upset? I like it when... people... just vanish without a word—all—the—time."

Charlie kicked at the bottom step of the porch. "Would it help if I said I was sorry?"

Nina turned her back on him, unlocked the door and pushed it all the way open with her foot. "Not really," she said. "I've heard it too many times by now." She walked the rest of the way into the house. He was probably following right after her again, and she wouldn't give him the satisfaction of getting all startled again at having him three inches behind her—so there.

But she couldn't hear his footfall as she was stomping down the hallway to the bedroom, pulling her suitcase behind her with the wheels rattling over the floor boards. And when she got into the bedroom and finally stole a glance over her shoulder, he wasn't there. Hmph. Disappeared again, had he? Yeah, that was annoying. But then, she wasn't going to think about him anymore, was she? No, she wasn't. So there. Even when he had just been right outside. Nina yanked her suitcase up onto the bed with an angry little thump, clicked open the latches and threw back the top.

She'd at least put on a clean T-shirt, that's what she'd do. Rifling through the clothes, she found one—her favourite bright green Kermit shirt, which had nothing but the frog's eyes and mouth on it and you still instantly knew who it was. She started to unbutton her blouse—but wait, he-who-she-wasn't-thinking-about might still be coming down the hall. Or looking in the window. She wouldn't put it past him! A small corner of her mind was telling her that now she was being unfair, not to mention ridiculous, but she didn't listen to it. She was mad, and that was that! She stomped to the window and pulled the curtains shut with a vicious yank, making the curtain rings rattle, then slammed the bedroom door shut as well and for good measure pushed in the lock in the door handle. She vaguely considered jamming the chair that stood in the corner of the room under the door handle, but now the voice in her head told her she was skirting dangerously close to being a jerk herself, and she didn't want to hear that. The voice was right—Charlie was actually a polite guy. He wouldn't be such a creep as to walk into a girl's bedroom when she had obviously closed the door on him—would he?

As it turned out, he wasn't even in the house. Nina came out of her bedroom feeling quite a bit calmer than when she had gone in, so she was ready to meet Charlie with equanimity, but there was no Charlie in the living room to practice her benevolence on. Nor was he in the kitchen. Finally Nina threw a glance outside through the window over the couch, which looked out onto the porch. There he was, still at the bottom of the porch steps, leaning against the trunk of the tree, his arms folded over his chest and a grouchy—no, forlorn—look on his face.

Oh, whatever!

Nina pulled open the half-closed front door. Charlie looked up, and his blue eyes lit up with something that looked like hope. Nina's heart gave a little skip. He was awfully cute when he looked at her with that little-boy-lost expression on his face... But no, she was still mad at him! She hardened her heart, blue eyes or not. But he might as well come in.

She pulled up an eyebrow. "So, are you just going to stand around there? Is my humble cottage not nice enough for you to deign to set foot in?"

A half-doubtful, half-eager smile crept across his face. "Are you inviting me in?"

Nina rolled her eyes again. "Uh, yeah? Do you want it in writing, cream laid paper, RSVP ASAP? Sorry, not happening; I'm a bit short on postage stamps at the moment."

She stepped back from the door as he pretty much bounded up onto the porch and bounced across the threshold. Once again he stood only three inches in front of her, staring down into her face with that serious, inscrutable expression in his eyes, and Nina found herself catching her breath.

"Thanks for inviting me in," he said, as if she had conferred this massive favour on him.

She started breathing again, with a slight effort. "Uh, yeah, whatever." Why was it such a big deal to him to have to be *invited* to come in? He popped in and out of her garden readily enough.

Nina pushed the door shut and skirted around him, stepping into the living room. "Well, guess what," she said, and she could hear that she was babbling nervously, "I got into my car. *By myself.*" So there, she barely stopped herself from adding.

His eyebrows jumped, and there was a disappointed look in his eyes. "Well, hurrah for you," he said, and it sounded like it cost him a slight effort to say it.

"Hmph," she said, "no thanks to you."

"I know," he said quietly. "I'm s—"

"Oh, enough already," Nina said. She plopped herself down on the couch. "However, I'm still not out of the woods. Turns out my phone is out of charge, and I've forgotten my USB charger. You don't happen to have a USB-C cable I could borrow? I know you don't have a cell phone, but it's the same charger as a lot of tablets use, or wireless headsets or stuff like that."

He shook his head. "I'm afraid not," he said. "Kind of short on technology."

"Hmm." Nina made a face. "I guess I'll have to go to town then. Does Houghton have a store where I could get something like this?"

Charlie shrugged. "Possibly?"

"What do you mean? 'Possibly there is a store' or 'possibly they have a USB cable phone charger'?"

"The latter," he said quickly, "definitely the latter."

Nina had the distinct feeling that he actually had meant the former.

"Hmph. Well, I guess I'll have to go find out. So how do I actually get to this place?"

"To Houghton? Down the road, turn left, take the first left again, go for a bit, then right for a couple of miles, left at the fork, right at the T-junction, north for a mile and a half, and you're there."

"Uh—say what?" Remembering directions had never been Nina's strong suit. "I think I need that in writing." Pen and paper, was there some pen and paper? "Hey, do you know if there's a piece of paper around somewhere?"

"Move your feet." Charlie grabbed the edge of the coffee table box that Nina had her feet propped up on. Nina swung her feet down, and he lifted the lid. "Here you go," he said, reaching in and handing Nina a couple of sheets of paper.

Nina got her purse and pulled out her black clicky souvenir ballpoint from BC Ferries with the little ship in a bottle in the shaft. "Write it down," she said, giving the sheet of paper back to Charlie and handing him the pen as well.

He looked at the pen. "That's neat," he said, tipping the pen back and forth to make the little flat ferry "sail" back and forth.

"Uh, yeah," Nina said. She was fond of that pen; it reminded her of Vancouver Island, which was one of her most favourite places on earth. "So, the directions please?"

He started writing, then he quit again. "Here, this would be easier." He flipped the paper over and drew some straight lines. "This is this street, Hawthorn Lane. We're here,"—he drew a little square box—"and this is, uh, Jade—I mean, the other house, where you saw the bear. Keep going until the end of the road, take a left. Go down the next left, keep going for a bit until you get to a right turn. Then..."

He kept drawing rights and lefts until Nina was thoroughly confused. But she had the map. She only had to imagine his voice going "In. Two Hundred. Metres. Turn left," and she'd be okay. Except hearing his voice in her head might be a bit distracting...

"All right, thanks," she said when he finished his masterpiece of cartography by drawing a couple of little kindergarten-style houses and neatly labelled them "Houghton." She stood up from the couch and picked up her purse, holding out her hand for the map. "I might as well get going—I need to get into my phone and figure out what my boss wanted. I know she kept calling me and texting me; that's probably what drained the battery on my phone so fast."

Charlie rose as well. He held out the map—then he drew it back again.

"Nina," he said, looking at her intently, "what if I told you I can't help it?"

Lost

Nina shook her head as she shifted her car into third gear. Charlie was trying to make her believe that his disappearing and reappearing was not something that happened from his own volition. Yeah, right. Like she was going to buy that he just popped in and out of existence? As if it was some kind of magic? She wasn't having any. If the guy kept hopping in and out of her life and her house, at least he could admit to it. But the funny thing was that he hadn't sounded like he was trying to have her on, but as if he was serious about it. Believed it himself, even. What did that make him, delusional? It was weird though—his being delusional was about as likely as all of this happening by magic. He seemed like an eminently sane person.

Well, whatever. Nina hadn't believed him—wasn't believing him. She hadn't even let him finish, but taken the map he had drawn and left—sort of like he was always doing... Well, not quite. At least she had said good-bye. She'd kind of had to—she wasn't going to leave him in the house; so she had made him get outside so she could lock the door. She felt a little guilty thinking of the disappointed look in his eyes, or sad, or whatever that look had been. But she wasn't willing to forgive him for walking out on her the way he was doing all the time, and then trying to blame it on some kind of woo-woo mystical stuff. Which was also why she hadn't asked him to come along for the ride to give her directions. Not that he would have come anyway—or he probably would have done another bunk.

Nina stepped on the clutch and shifted back down to second gear. "At the end of the road, turn left," the Charlie Maps navigator said in her mind's ear. All right, left it was. That's where she had been heading when the deluge hit the day before. There, that's how far she had gotten that time. So after this, it was unknown territory.

"Okay, what's next?" Nina said out loud. "A right? No, that isn't right, it has to be another another left. Right?" Nina chuckled as she heard herself saying all this. She slowed down the car and cast a glance at the map lying beside her on the passenger seat. Yes, "Take the first left," he'd said. Nina kept the car at a crawl, looking along the left side of the road for a turn-off. There wasn't another soul on this road anyway, so it wasn't like she was blocking anybody's way by going 25 km/h.

There were trees by the side of the road. And more trees. Talking about not seeing the wood for trees... Ah, what was this? Yes, that looked like a turn-off. Not a very wide one, but it was definitely a road. Paved, even, unlike Hawthorn Lane. Nina put on the indicator and made a left. It was a narrow road, hemmed in by looming pine trees, winding through the woods.

"To grandmother's house we go," Nina muttered. "Just have to watch for the Big Bad Wolf."

After a few hundred metres the road took a sharp right. Nina glanced over at her map. Was that what Charlie had meant by "take a right"? She shrugged. It wasn't like she had anywhere else to go. Even turning the car around would be tricky on this road.

Somehow Nina didn't think that this was the route Google Maps had shown her, back when her phone was still working. She remembered it being more straight-forward, and the roads hadn't looked as tiny as this, either. She gave a sigh and then a yawn. "Coffee," she muttered, "I could really use a coffee about now." Maybe there was some to be had in Houghton? Actually, almost guaranteed there was. What town didn't have a coffee shop, or at least a gas station that sold coffee? Drinking tea in the quantities she'd been doing was all fine and dandy, but sometimes a girl needed something stronger.

The paved road ended abruptly, gravel paths going off to the right and left. Hmm—left at the fork, Charlie'd said? This wasn't really a fork, per se, but there hadn't *been* anything that could be called a fork. Nina turned left. The car was bumping along the gravel road at 20 km/h, then even that seemed too fast as the gravel ended and all that was left were a couple of wheel ruts through the trees.

This couldn't be right—no way was this the road to town. That junction had to have been the T, not the fork, in which case she should have gone right. Or had she?

It was hard enough keeping her rights and lefts straight without the roads winding and turning and getting all narrow and dirt-roady, to boot.

Nina stopped and put the car in reverse. A ten-point-turn later (back and forth by inches, so as not to get stuck on the tree trunks lying by the side of the road) she had the car's nose pointed back in the direction she'd come from. North for a mile and a half after the T, right? Wherever north was—the compass in her cell phone only worked if the phone was on. Which it wasn't.

The car slowly bumped along the path, scaring a squirrel that darted out of the way and then sat by the side of the road, angrily chittering at Nina.

"Pooh to you, too," Nina said to it. "I'd rather be out on the Trans-Canada, myself, not rattling around here in the woods, frightening small critters."

The path—it still wasn't much more than that—took a sudden S-curve. What? Had she already passed the spot where she had gotten onto this road, where the paving ended and the dirt road began? Apparently she had, because she could not remember that S-curve. Whatever, she wasn't going to turn around again.

Another bend in the road, this one a sharp left. And there was the town! Or, wait, no. That wasn't the town; all it was was a house. A single house, sitting in the woods. With pink siding, tall windows and gingerbread trim. How many pink houses *were* there in this neighbourhood? This one looked exactly like that neighbour's house, except it had its porch wrapped around it on the back side, and a garage jutting out front.

But there was something off about this place. Something that made Nina uneasy. Maybe it was the trees. They seemed really dark here, sort of looming, black. And that house, for all its pink frilliness, looked like a spider sitting in a web, waiting for its victim.

Or maybe it reminded Nina too much of that other house, of her encounter with the bear. If this had been the same house, the bear would have come from... Wait a minute. *Was* this another house?

Nina stopped the car, put the gear shift in neutral, pulled the handbrake, and half stepped out of the car, looking around.

This was the same house. Without a doubt. She must have gotten lost, taken a wrong turn somewhere, and here she was coming at the place from its backside. The place that she had promised Charlie not to go near again—or had she? He'd been very adamant about it. But then, it wasn't like she had any responsibility to him, so, really... And Nina *had* to get to town. But maybe the people here had a phone charger they could loan her? If there were people there at all, that was.

Nina made up her mind and stepped all the way out of the car. But no—she wasn't going to do the same stupid twice in a row! She ducked back into the car, turned off the ignition, pulled out the key and stuck it in her pocket. Her gaze fell on her open purse on the passenger seat. The pink dog spray bottle on its little chain was slipping out of the bag. Right. This was Mr. Bear's house. This time she would be prepared.

Dog spray in hand, her finger on the trigger, she stepped out of the car. There was a door on this side of the house. She'd give it a try, see if anyone was home.

She made it no more than a dozen steps. There was a movement, a crashing in the bushes—Nina gasped, her heart felt like it wanted to leap from her chest—and there was the bear, coming right at her!

Nina pushed the trigger.

The dog spray blew out in a cloud, hitting the animal full in the face. He reared up, roared, pawed at his nose—Nina rushed back, threw herself in the car and slammed the door. Her fingers trembling so hard she could barely move them, she fumbled for her keys, shoved them in the ignition, cranked on the engine, slammed the gear into reverse and backed away. Out of the corner of her eye she saw the bear lumbering off into the trees—then she was fifty metres down the forest road, the house and bear out of sight.

Nina stopped the car and clutched the steering wheel, shaking all over. She put her forehead down onto her clenched hands and breathed deeply, nearly hyperventilating.

That bear again. Always that bear. And the house. What was it with that house, and that bear? It was like he didn't want her getting to the house. But he was an animal—what did he know about houses?

Nina was so shaken she had a hard time getting the car put into gear. She nosed the vehicle around, and carefully drove back the way she had come. This time, she did not overshoot the turnoff where the paving began, and she slowly rolled down the curving road.

What had Charlie been thinking, giving her these directions? This was simply *wrong*. He had been so sure, though...

Nina reached the turning to the bigger road. So the cottage was off to the right. But she still did not have her phone charge cable, and she was running low on gas. If she didn't find a gas station soon, she'd be in trouble.

She turned onto the road, and five hundred metres later, was met with a most welcome sight: a road led off to the left, with a sign proclaiming in large white letters on green ground: Houghton 5 km.

Left. The *second* road to the left, not the first. What was Charlie's problem? Didn't he know his directions? Or was he dyslexic and couldn't count? Well, even dyslexics should be able to count to two...

In Town

Ten minutes later, Nina rolled into Houghton. Curiously enough, after that first mistake, all of Charlie's directions had been right. Not that she'd needed them, once she got on the right road—there were enough road signs to point the way.

Houghton proved to be a tiny, old-fashioned town that played up its pioneer history to the hilt, and seemed to consist of one main street running down the middle, ending in a park by the shore of a lake. It didn't quite have board walks running in front of the shops with their false facades, but they certainly wouldn't have been out of place. A second-hand bookstore, a bakery, an IGA grocery store, two coffee shops right across from each other, a bakery, a hardware store, a drugstore, a pub, and about three "ye olde gifte shoppes" vied for the hapless tourist's attention.

"Well, *this* tourist needs a cup of coffee," Nina muttered. "And then a gas station, and a phone charge cable. In that order."

She angle-parked her Toyota in front of "Koffee and Krumble," which was right next to "Once Upon a Tyme Pre-Read Books," collected her purse, and got out. In spite of the twee name, the coffee shop looked inviting. They had some delicious-looking pastries displayed in the window, and when the door opened to let out a couple of elderly ladies with shopping bags, a mouth-watering scent of cinnamon buns wafted out into the street. Nina heaved a blissful sigh—this was what she'd been after.

It turned out that the bookstore was not only right beside the coffee shop, it was actually connected to it with a big open doorway between the buildings—they were one store, really. The knotty-pine panelling on the walls carried through right into the bookshop, its Ye Olde Frontier vibe reinforced by the framed black-and-white photos hung all around the room. Probably pictures of the town's history.

Nina collected her very twenty-first-century caramel macchiato from the counter and chose a table next to the doorway to the bookshop. Glancing around the corner, she noticed that the picture frames in the shop mostly contained yellowed newspaper cuttings, several of them showing the headline of "Houghton Herald"—the local newsrag, apparently.

She cupped her hands around her mug, took a sip, and closed her eyes in bliss as the flavour rolled over her tongue. She'd needed this. Aaah.

"Miss? Were you the Cindy's Cinnamon Swirl Delight with extra icing?"

Nina's eyes popped open. The teenaged barista stood in front of her, holding a plate with a steaming brown pinwheel bun that gave off the most mouth-watering scent.

"Yes! Ooh, thank you."

"There you are then," the girl said with a bright smile, "enjoy!" With a flourish, she deposited the plate in front of Nina. "So, you on a holiday then?"

Nina raised her eyebrows. "Why, do I have 'tourist' written on my forehead?"

The teenager laughed. "No need for that. You're a stranger, that's enough."

"I suppose you know everyone in town?"

"You bet I do. When there's only 500—no, sorry, 493—people in the town, you literally know everybody. And I mean *everybody*. *All* your life. I can't wait to get out of here when I graduate..." she said wistfully.

"Where are you planning to go?"

"Oh, I dunno—Calgary, Vancouver—anywhere so long as it's bigger than here. Even Kelowna would do in a pinch; I've got a cousin there."

"Vancouver is nice," Nina said, "that's where I'm from. Lived there all my life. The rain in winter gets tedious though."

"Yeah, that's what I hear," the girl said. "But I think I could put up with it. The snow here gets old too."

"By the looks of it, 'old' is something you do well here," Nina said, gesturing at the black-and-white prints on the wall.

"Tell me about it," the girl said, casually leaning back against the neighbouring table and folding her arms, settling in for a chat. "You get kind of sick of local history around here. History and trees, that's all we got."

"And bears, don't forget bears," Nina said with a shudder.

"Yeah, those too. Why, you seen one?"

"Oh yeah, you could say that!" Nina opened her eyes wide and pursed her lips. "Twice! Right on the street where my—where the house is where I'm staying."

"That's weird," the girl said. "I haven't heard of one hanging around close to town this summer. Black or grizzly?"

"Uh—black, I think. I was so freaked out I didn't bother googling it at the time. And I don't know how 'close' this is, where I saw him—it's quite a ways out there, in the woods. About eight klicks."

"Oh yeah?" The girl raised her eyebrows. "Didn't know there was a B&B outside of town. Who's running it then?"

"It's not exactly a B&B," Nina said. She took a bite of her cinnamon bun. "Boy, this is good!"

"Yeah, Cindy's an awesome baker," the girl said. "So you staying with friends?"

"No," Nina said. "Actually,"—she brightened as a thought occurred to her—"you're local and know everybody, you'll be able to tell me!"

"Tell you what?" The girl hitched up her skinny jeans and pulled down her fluorescent green tank top, exposing a little extra cleavage.

"Okay, so here's the scoop: I inherited this house—cottage, whatever. But I don't really know who the person is I got it from. It's out on Hawthorn Lane; the lady was called Miranda—Miranda McManus."

The barista wrinkled her forehead and pulled on the long blonde braid that swung over one shoulder.

"Miranda McManus? Miranda McManus. Hmm. I mean, I know *everybody*, but that name doesn't ring a bell, not offhand. When did you say she died?"

"I didn't, because I don't know. Judging by the state of the garden, it might have been a while ago. Or maybe she was sick and just let the garden go? The house is clean enough, so maybe she only died recently—maybe that's what happened. So you've never heard of her?"

"Actually, wait. Wait wait wait wait," the girl said. She whirled around, her braid swinging, shaking her finger at one after the other of the prints on the wall. "This... this this this... Nooo, no, not that—shoot, where was it?" She disappeared next door into the bookshop. "Hey Jerry," Nina could hear her voice, "where's that article about that community fete, you know, from way back when, about the lady with the strawberries?"

A man's voice answered. "Which lady, the one that won all the prizes, like, five years in a row, back in the eighties?"

"Yeah, yeah, you know, in the big gold frame."

"I think it's back..." The voices moved farther away, and Nina could no longer make them out.

A couple of minutes later the girl was back, carrying a large-ish picture frame, which she laid in front of Nina.

"Look," she said, "I knew I'd seen that name somewhere." She pointed at the article in the frame.

"McManus Takes Fifth Win in a Row," the headline on the yellowed paper said. Underneath was a grainy newspaper photo of an older lady with short, light-coloured hair—blonde, light grey, white?—holding out a basket with what looked like strawberries, a great big ribbon with a "1" in the centre pinned to the basket. She had a beaming smile on her face, and Nina thought she looked really nice. There was something about her that reminded her of Granny.

"Houghton's annual garden club show once again boasts some impressive wins. The top prize is carried off by Miranda McManus, whose strawberries came in top of the category..."

Nina looked for when that article was printed, but it had been cut from the middle of the newspaper page, and there was no date in sight.

"Aren't these really old articles?" she asked the girl.

"Yeah, I'm pretty sure that one's from the eighties!"

"No—I meant 'old' old, like pioneer stuff, you know, turn of the last century, that kind of thing."

"Like, historical? No, not all of them. There's a few, but the rest of them Cindy made up to look like that—pseudo-antique, you know. It sells better with the tourists. Umm, sorry—no offence."

"That's okay," Nina said. She gazed at the photo of Miranda McManus and her strawberries. She could attest to the quality of those berries, if they were from the vines she still had in her garden.

"Like, a lot of those pictures on the wall here," the girl continued, "weren't really black and white to start with—like I said, eighties, and they did have colour photos then. I know, cause that's when my mom and dad were kids, and they have colour photos of themselves. Cindy had some of the photos copied and printed black and white." She picked up the frame and turned it over. "Yeah, look," she said, pointing at a pencilled date on the back. "It's from July 1989."

The bell over the door of the coffee shop rang and a man and two women came in.

"Oh, gotta go," the barista said. She turned to the new customers. "What can I get started for you?"

Nina thoughtfully finished her cinnamon bun. The Miranda lady must have been really old when she died, if this photo was from the late eighties—she already looked elderly in it, and that was more than thirty years ago.

Nina took a sip from her latté and let her gaze travel around the room. So those old-looking photos weren't actually old, were they? She took a closer look at the one that was hanging on the wall beside her seat. It seemed to be a town parade going up the middle of Main Street—there was the café in the background. And sure enough, it had to be from sometime in the late eighties or maybe early nineties, as some of the spectators in the crowd still sported mullets and shoulder pads, but the girls all had sleek hair and swooping bangs—including the "Miss Houghton" who was riding prominently on the float in the middle. She had a massive, teased-up set of white-blonde bangs drooping over one eye, and was striking a provocative pose that looked, somehow, inappropriate. Nina wondered why there was something off about it—then she looked more closely and realized that the woman was actually not a young girl, but at least forty. She had a cougar-ish look about her, not attractive. Although, judging by the sappy look on the face of the guy in the front row of the spectators, male opinions on the matter differed from Nina's. Females, on the other hand, seemed to concur; there was one with a big sun hat on who had a particularly disgusted look on her face as she glared at the Miss Houghton. Hang on—wasn't that Miranda? Nina looked back to the newspaper photo, then up at the parade picture, then back at the article. Yes, that was definitely her! Interesting.

So if that was Miranda in the picture of the parade, Nina wondered if she was in any of the other photos. She twisted her head to look at the picture on the wall behind her chair—no, that was a bunch of loggers, by the looks of it an actual old photo—not "old" by the standards of a seventeen-year-old, but from probably the early 1900s. The one next to that was newer again, possibly the seventies, and showed a group of workers posing in front of a building by the lakeshore with a big sign on it saying "Houghton Fish Cannery". A fish cannery, this far inland? Nina'd thought they only existed at the coast. But then again, there were fish in lakes, too.

Nina picked up her purse and started wandering around the coffee shop. There weren't a lot of other customers, so she could get close enough to the walls to peer at the photos. There, that looked like Miranda again! Another garden club or village fete thing, by the looks of it; she was holding a bucket of apples that time. She looked a bit younger there than in the strawberry picture, her hair darker, so apparently she'd been around a while in that town. Interesting.

Nina went back to her table, tipped the last few sips of her now-lukewarm latté down her throat, and ran her finger around the plate to lick up the last sticky bits of cinnamon goo and icing. The cinnamon bun had been amazing—should she get one to go? She picked up her plate and cup and carried them to the counter, where the barista was serving a hipster-looking dude a non-fat soy double-shot venti something-or-other.

"And one of the butter tarts, please," the guy was saying. "Can I have whipped cream on that?"

"We don't have soy whip," the girl said, "is that okay?"

"Yeah, that's fine," he said, "but is it organic?"

"Umm," said the girl, "I think so?"

"Fantastic," the guy said, "my spirit is craving soft sweetness today." He gave the barista a smarmy smile. She raised her eyebrows a bit, served him his drink—in a disposable cup with a plastic lid—and popped the butter tart with its cap of whip into a to-go container.

When the bell over the door had rung his exit from the café, she turned to Nina and rolled her eyes.

"Non-fat soy milk," she said, "and then wants whipped cream—I ask you!"

"But it's organic!" Nina said facetiously.

The girl took an ordinary pink and white Dairyland whipping cream carton from the fridge under the counter and pretended to inspect it carefully. "Yup, definitely organic."

"As opposed to inorganic?" Nina said.

The girl grinned. "Exactly. I hate it when they try to hit on me with some organic vegan bullshit that they don't even mean."

"I hear you. Nothing wrong with organic or vegan—"

"Oh no! Not if you actually believe in it and carry it through. We have lots of old hippies in the back forty here, they're the real deal. They were doing that stuff way before it got trendy. But people like that guy…"

"Yes. We get that type in the Starbucks by my work."

"In Vancouver?" the girl asked eagerly. "I wonder if I could get a job there. I do have experience here."

"I bet you could," Nina said.

"Can I get you anything else?" the girl asked. "Like the carrot cake? It's vegan!" She giggled.

Nina grinned. "Actually, can you get me another one of those cinnamon buns to go?"

"Sure. It's three ninety-five."

Nina pulled her wallet out of her purse, and as she did so, looked at the print that hung behind and slightly to the left of the counter. It was a photo of half a dozen people sitting on the pedestal of the statue of Sir John A. MacDonald down by the boat launch, smiling at the photographer. There was Miranda again, and beside her—

"What??" Nina dropped her wallet to the floor, and her change spilled out, the nickels and dimes rolling over the dark tile floor. She stared at the picture. It couldn't be—it wasn't! But—

Nina squatted down to collect her runaway cash, but she kept looking up, staring at the photo.

The barista girl came around the counter. "Here, let me help you," she said, bending down to help Nina gather up her coins. She picked up Nina's wallet and held it out to her, then did a double-take. "Hey, are you okay?"

Nina gave her head a quick shake, then stood up and stepped closer to the photo. "I think so—no, I'm not sure; I just thought I recognized..."

"Who? Oh, that's that Miranda lady again you were talking about, from the article in the paper!"

"No, not her—the guy beside her. Him!" She pointed at the face. A young, dark-haired, bearded man in a plaid jacket, jeans and heavy work boots, smiling, his eyes crinkled up against the sun that was shining in his face.

Charlie.

"Oh, him! He's kind of cute, don't you think?" The girl giggled.

"*Who is he?*"

The girl shrugged and gave Nina the change she had collected from the floor. "Dunno—this is all from way before my time." She took the picture from the wall and pointed to the date on the back. "There, see, May 1995."

Nina shook her head. "It can't be—it doesn't make sense!" She shoved her wallet in her purse and reached out for the picture. "I *have* to know who he is!"

The girl gave her a quizzical look.

"Why?"

Nina pulled herself up short. "Well, uh, he—he looks like someone I know," she said lamely.

"Oh, okay," the girl said. She pointed her chin in the direction of the bookstore. "You could ask Jerry. He's way older than me, he knows all kinds of stuff about this town. Here, take the picture. I'll hang onto your Cinnamon Swirl Delight until you're ready to go. Oh, can you give him the article back, too? It belongs in the back corner of the store by the mangas, that's why I knew about it."

Nina only half heard the last part of that. She was clutching the picture frame and skirting around the little café tables as quickly as she could, scooping up the other frame on her way.

"Hi," she said, swinging around the doorway of the bookshop and coming to a stop in front of the sales counter that stood at right angles to the door. "What can you tell me about *this* guy?" She pointed at the picture of Charlie in the black and white photo.

Jerry turned out to be a man in his early forties, his sandy hair, which he wore in a scraggly ponytail, balding on top and greying at the sides. He glanced at Nina over a pair of half-moon glasses, then looked down at the photo.

"Oh, him!" There was a slight undertone of displeasure in his voice. "That's the guy who disappeared, wasn't it?"

Nina stared at him. "Disappeared?"

"Yeah." Jerry picked up the gold-framed article and started walking towards the back of the store with it, wending his way down the narrow aisle between the bookshelves that were tightly packed with old paperbacks and a few hardcovers.

Nina followed him. "What happened?"

"He was this English guy, showed up in town one day. Hung around for a while, did odd jobs for people. And then one day he up and vanished, that's all."

"Vanished how?"

"Not a clue." He hung up the frame with the article on a nail between two shelves crammed with graphic novels, then stepped back a pace and eyed it. "Jadice reported him missing." He said it as if it left a sour taste in his mouth. "But nothing ever came of it; the guy never showed up again." He stepped back to the article and straightened it by a few millimetres.

"Who is Jadice?" Nina had to back up against the book shelf as he pushed his way past her to the front of the store.

"She used to live around here—outside of town, towards Hambleton." He vaguely waved his hand in the direction that Nina had driven into town from, and stepped back behind his sales counter. "She was—she was something else." His eye took on a dreamy expression, and a slight smile played around his mouth. "Beautiful. Long blonde hair, a figure to die for... She was a real woman, you know? A *mature* woman. Actually," he squinted at the photo still lying on the counter, "that's her right there!" His voice took on an excited tone, and he stabbed his finger at a figure on the far left of the picture. He picked up the frame and held it close to his face. "Yes, that's definitely her! I didn't know Cindy had a picture of her in the store! I'll have to get a copy of that. See?" He turned the photo around and held it out to Nina.

Nina looked at the person in the picture. She had long blonde hair all right, and was showing off that figure Jerry had mentioned in a skin-tight tank top. In fact, it was the woman who was so patently demonstrating her assets in the picture of the parade.

Nina wondered if those assets were entirely natural, then mentally slapped herself on the wrist for being judgemental.

"Wasn't she Miss Houghton at some point?"

"Yes!" he said excitedly. "In '93, '94, *and* '95! She should have had it in '96 too, but... How did you know?"

"There's a picture of it, on the wall right around the corner here." Nina pointed at the wall beside the sales desk.

"No way, really? Why didn't I know that?" He scooted out from behind the desk.

"No idea," Nina said, blocking his way. "So, uh, about this English guy—she reported him missing?"

"Yeah," he said sourly. "She went to the RCMP and told them she'd been expecting him to do a job on her house, but he never showed. She blamed Miranda McManus, said she'd know about it, but Miranda refused to say anything. Figures."

"You knew Miranda?"

"'Course. She was Jade's neighbour."

Was she indeed? So Jadice had to be the owner of the pink house with resident bear!

"Um, does Jadice still live here? Is she at home?"

A shadow crossed Jerry's face. "No. She's been gone for a long time now. Like I said, she should have had the Miss Houghton crown in '96, too, but they gave it to Tracy Miller instead. As if!" He scoffed. "Trace couldn't hold a candle to Jadice. She was just a green kid; we graduated together. So she was only seventeen. She had none of that ripe beauty Jadice had." He sighed. "I think Jade felt so hurt she couldn't stand it in this town anymore. You can't really blame her; she didn't feel appreciated. Then one day this city guy showed up in a fancy car, some lawyer or businessman or something, she knew him from before she came here, and she left with him. I think they were going snowbirding, move to Florida or whatever. She said she'd stay in touch, but..." He pushed his way past Nina. "Where is this picture you said Cindy had?"

Nina pointed through the doorway to the coffee shop, and he vanished through it.

Nina's head was in a whirl. Disappeared in 1996. It made no sense. But what about his constant vanishing act at the cottage? He couldn't help it, he said...

Nina picked up a book from a stack of identical volumes on the counter—*Houghton Sesqui-Centenary 1862-2012*, it said on the cover over a sepia photo of a paddle wheeler. Unthinkingly, Nina started riffling through the pages. It looked like it was an illustrated history of the town—"History and trees, that's all we've got," the young barista's voice echoed in Nina's mind. There were sepia-coloured photos of the early history of the town: the paddle wheeler that used to take passengers down to the train station at the far end of the lake; log floats that went the same way; the hotel that was where the IGA now stood...

"Are you going to buy a copy of that?" Jerry's voice asked. "It's twenty-five bucks."

He was sidling back in behind his counter, hugging a picture frame to his chest. Nina recognized it as the one that had hung beside her seat in the café.

"Yeah, I guess," she said, flipping through the book some more. "Oh, there's Miranda!" It was the garden club photo with the old lady holding the strawberries, except it was in colour here, which showed that her hair was definitely white, not blonde.

"Oh yeah, she's in there," Jerry said, ringing up the sale. The cash drawer opened with a *Pring!* and he pushed it shut again, handing Nina the debit machine instead.

"So was she really prominent in this town, or what?" Nina punched in her PIN, waited for the screen to notify her that the payment was accepted, then pulled her credit card back out of the machine.

"Yeah, I guess," Jerry said, slipping the book and receipt into a flat paper bag. "Had her fingers in all the pies when it came to gardening and growing stuff. We used to think she was a witch when we were kids." He laughed, then his forehead drew down in a frown. "Mind you, after what happened with that English guy, I wouldn't be surprised..."

Nina raised her eyebrows. "You mean with him disappearing?"

"Yeah, like I said, Jade said Miranda had something to do with it. And I believe her."

Of course he did.

"But she wouldn't say anything, so the RCMP dropped it and put him on a missing persons list. They had posters up for a while, and then they gave up. It wasn't like anyone else was looking for him either—you know, like desperate moms going on TV and handing out flyers everywhere. So he stayed missing, I guess. I don't think Jadice missed him either—at least she didn't look like she did. I was kind of hoping..." He trailed off.

He'd been seventeen, and that woman, what, forty? Eew.

"She did report him disappearing though, didn't she?"

"Yes, well, she was an honourable person that way—you know, public-spirited. That's why it was so hard for her when she didn't get the Miss Houghton crown. Contributing to the community is an important part of that."

"I suppose the other girl—what was her name, Lacy?—"

"Tracy."

"—yes, I suppose she contributed too?"

He looked huffy. "They made a big deal of her being the first girl to volunteer for the fire department," he said. "But still, Jadice..."

Nina barely kept herself from letting out a snort. Volunteering in the fire department, as a seventeen-year-old girl, would beat out pretty much *any* other contender, physical beauty notwithstanding. And Nina was willing to bet that a nice, natural teen girl had an aging botox beauty beat in the looks department, too. But she wasn't about to say so to this guy who was still hankering after said aging botox beauty twenty-odd years later. Not if she wanted more actual information from the guy.

"So, Jerry," she said, "tell me more about Miranda. How long did she live here?"

"Well, as long as I can remember," he said, "until she died, of course. Or did she move away? I can't remember."

"When was that?"

"I dunno, sometime in the nineties, I think."

In the nineties? But...

"Was this before or after Jade—Jadice left?"

"Oh, after. I wish it had been before, then maybe Jade would have stayed..."

"Why?"

"They didn't get along."

Now there was a surprise—not. What Nina was starting to learn about these women made her inclined to agree with Miranda in the matter.

"So you don't know what happened to Miranda?"

"No, not really. She just quit coming into town. Or, actually—wait a sec." He scratched the back of his head, pulling some strands of hair loose from his ponytail. "I think she left some stuff with George first. So she probably actually left instead of dying."

"Who's George?"

"George Harmon, he's the notary public. I remember him saying something a couple of weeks ago—or a month maybe—that it was time to mail that thing Miranda had given him."

Nina's head came up. "Mail what thing?"

"I dunno. Some fat brown envelope. I think it was going to a lawyer's firm in Vancouver, from what I saw of the address."

"He showed it to you?" Or had Jerry been snooping in someone else's mail?

"No, we were just at the post office at the same time, so I saw it. George said he'd had it sitting in his safe ever since Miranda left, with the instruction to mail it out about now."

A fat brown envelope, going to Vancouver. A *lawyers's firm* in Vancouver. Nina was willing to bet anything that it was Spreckles, Masters and Mifflin, that lawyer's firm. And that the envelope had contained the will and the house key that had sent Nina herself hotfooting it out here to claim her inheritance. But none of it answered the question *why* Miranda had left her property to Nina.

"Anyway, is there anything else I can do for you?" Jerry picked up the framed print again and hugged it to his chest. "'Cause if not, I'm gonna, you know, see about getting this copied." He gazed down at the photo with a longing look in his eyes. He'd probably get it blown up so that all you could see was Miss Botox Beauty.

Nina had had about enough of him. She might have to come back some other time and get some more information out of him—or maybe she would go see the George guy instead—but for now, she wanted to get out of there.

"No, that's okay. Thanks for the info and the book." She hoisted the paper bag in her hand. "Can you point me in the direction of the gas station?"

Fired

Nina looked down at her phone in shock. It had taken a full twenty minutes for the darn thing to charge enough to be able to open it and check her emails, while she kept driving the roads of Backwoods Nowheresville, aka the forest around Houghton, to keep the cigarette lighter—sorry, the 12V outlet—charging without draining the car battery. And now here she was, parked by the side of the road, the subject line of her boss's email staring her in the face: "YOU'RE FIRED!!!!!!!"

With shaking fingers, she tapped the flaming letters to open the mail, and in spite of already knowing what it was going to say, she flinched at seeing the vitriol that spattered out at her from June's mail. Fired without notice, effective yesterday. While the phone was lying dead on the floor of the car, and Nina was tangling with ravenous bears in the woods.

Typical. So very typical. Nina should have expected this, but somehow, she hadn't. Hadn't even thought of it. But of course it had happened. This was what June did, fire people on the slightest pretext. The last girl got the shaft because she kept forgetting the exact Starbucks order June wanted—she would get a double shot skinny grande caramel macchiato instead of a triple. After the third time, June gave her the boot. And the guy who had the job before her apparently came to work one day with his shirt collar unbuttoned, which June interpreted as unwanted sexual advances—she had accused him of trying to show off his hairy chest. Nina had met the guy; a more hairless and inoffensive man was hard to imagine. She was sure that sexual advances to the boss had been the farthest thing from his mind. But June wanted to fire him, so that was that.

It was a miracle that Nina herself had hung on to the job this long in the first place, but somehow she still had not expected this. But there it was—because she hadn't been answering June's phone calls in the last couple of days, her job had gone down the drain. Poof. Kaputt. The fact that it was supposed to be Nina's time off didn't matter. A dozen progressively more irate emails from June, and then this.

In a daze, Nina turned on the ignition of the car, shifted into gear, and rolled down the road. The trees on either side of the road became blurry as her eyes filled with tears. It wasn't exactly that she had actually *liked* that job, let alone her boss. But it was a job—a body needed work, an income... You had to eat, and you had to have a roof over your head and wheels under your feet. None of which came free. And a job at a law firm was what she was qualified for. She had lived in Greater Vancouver all her life, that's what she knew, so she had never considered looking anywhere else. So now what was she going to do? Back to Van, back to trawling the job boards at the EI site and Kijiji and *The Province*. It sounded so unutterably dreary and depressing. Fortunately, she had a couple of months' worth of savings—a little bit of a cushion—but it couldn't last for ever...

Nina blinked and dashed the tears from her cheeks. Even on an empty country road it wasn't a good idea to drive without seeing where you were going. You might run yourself into the ditch, or have a collision with a flippin' *bear*. She gave a dispirited sniff and looked around. Where was she? No idea. The forest around her looked completely unfamiliar. Oh God—was she lost again?

Nina tried to pull herself together, stopped the car, and got out. She looked around, back behind her. Still no recognition. Damn.

But, oh, wait. Google Maps! She climbed back into the car, picked up her phone, and booted up the app. She still had the location of the cottage saved in the program, the little yellow star twinkling at her. Nina hit the blue "Directions" button and waited. The screen blurred as her tears started flowing again. It wasn't fair!

Through the blur of her tears she saw the "Start" button and tapped it.

"Go north. For five. Hundred metres," Google Maps instructed her.

North? Nina gave an angry titter. Where the heck was north? Google Maps was as bad as Charlie. She shifted the car out of neutral, let out the handbrake and started down the road.

"Make. A U-turn," Google Maps said, "then. Go north. For five. Hundred metres."

Go figure—she was going south. Stupid Google Maps, didn't know where you were until you started moving. She gave a little sob, slammed on the brake, yanked the gear shift into reverse, and turned around.

"You have arrived at. Your destination," the navigator cheerily informed her five minutes later.

"I know, damn you! Shut up!" Nina said angrily. She grabbed the phone and was about to yank the phone cord from the charger when she changed her mind. It was only 15% charged so far; best leave it on for a little while longer. It wasn't like she could charge it in the house. She stuck the phone on the dash, picked up her purse, the paper bag with the cinnamon bun, and the bag from IGA with the groceries she had picked up in town, and pushed her way through the gate in the hedge.

The thorn snagged her on the T-shirt again, just briefly, as if to say "Hi, welcome back!" Nina sniffed. At least the prickly hedge of liked her.

She dumped the groceries and the cinnamon bun in the kitchen and deposited her purse on the coffee table crate in the living room. Her eye fell on the pieces of paper that Charlie had left lying around on the top. With a sniff, she picked them up. Couldn't even clean up, that guy. Hmph. She lifted the lid of the box to stick the papers back in—but hang on. She'd never actually taken a proper look into that box. What else was in there? She sat down on the couch, pushed the lid of the crate all the way back and propped it open.

Paper—plain paper, some white, another pack slightly greyish or buff coloured with little darker specks in it. Nina picked up that paper and riffled through it. Some sheets lower down the stack had a fancy border printed around it, apparently stationery for writing letters, made from recycled paper. She moved to put the paper back into the box, and her eye fell on a book that had been underneath the paper. Largish, square, leather-covered. It looked exactly like... She dropped the paper and picked up the book.

Sure enough, it was a photo album.

Pictures

The album looked exactly like one Nina's grandmother used to have, with padded brown leather covers, about a foot square. Granny's had had see-through plastic sheets over sticky pages that you put the picture on and covered again with the plastic sheeting; it had been terrible on the photos. Nina still had it at home, but the pictures had gone kind of brown and started to disintegrate. She opened this album. No, this was different. The inside pages were plain white, with pages of tissue paper between them, the pictures stuck on with those clear photo corners. Good for Miranda, she had more respect for her pictures. If it *was* Miranda's album; though who else should it belong to?

And sure enough, the very first picture was one Nina recognized—Miranda with the strawberries, about three different versions of the photo in colour. The next page had the newspaper article pasted to it, and underneath, written in a spiky hand, "Seascape, excellent quality." Nina turned the page. Miranda with the garden club. Miranda, her hair still red-blond, sitting at an outdoor café table under a big sun umbrella, a man with a blond moustache and a sky blue suit with enormously long corners on his shirt collar sitting across from her, giving her a besotted look. The picture looked like it was from the seventies, judging by the man's clothes and the sort of washed-out colours and format of the print. Then there was Miranda wearing a straw hat, smiling at the camera—that one showed her in a garden with a hoe in her hand, between neat planter boxes overflowing with flowers and vegetables. Wait—that was *the* garden! There was the cottage in the background, the patio clearly visible, and the French doors standing open. The garden looked so nice—not tidy exactly, but as if the tangle of plants was entirely intentional, as well as confined to certain places. Nina recognized the apple tree, though it was much smaller, and there were the raspberry bushes along the fence—there *was* a fence, also quite tidy and solid-looking.

It was so different from that overgrown mess the garden was in at the moment... She'd really have to do something about that. Nina looked up through the French doors—and she jumped.

There stood Charlie on the patio, looking in at her.

Nina huffed air out of her nose. He hadn't been there a minute ago! Where did the guy *come* from? And why couldn't he have the courtesy to knock and let her know he was there?

She marched over to the French doors and pulled them open, then did a double-take.

Charlie looked terrible. His eyes were swollen nearly shut, tears running out of the corners; his face was flushed, his nose was running, and he kept breaking into a hacking cough like his lungs wanted to burst.

"What the heck have you done to yourself?" Nina asked.

"It's aller—allergies," he mumbled through this swollen lips, and dissolved into a coughing fit.

"To what?" Nina held open the door and stepped aside. "Come on in already. How long have you been standing there?"

"Not long," he croaked, stumbling into the house. "Thanks. I was hoping you'd let me in..."

"You look like hell." Her irritation with him got entirely swallowed up in concern. "Is there anything I can do for you? A cup of tea or something?"

He groaned. "Yes, please, a cuppa..."

"Have you seen an allergist about this?" Nina asked over her shoulder as she headed for the kitchen. "Is it environmental, or what?"

"Don't know—pepper, I think."

"What, like black pepper? A food allergy? Why do you put it on your food then?"

He coughed. "Please, tea..." He collapsed onto the couch, his hands pressed over his eyes.

Nina changed directions, went to the bathroom and wet a washcloth. On second thought, she also grabbed a roll of toilet paper. "Here, that might help," she said, coming back into the living room. She held out the washcloth to

Charlie, but he sat there clutching his face and didn't see. She took hold of his hand, pulled it away from his eyes and put the washcloth into it. "Try it, at least it's a bit cooler. And here's some Kleenex on a roll for your nose." She put the toilet paper on the coffee table box, then crouched down beside him, looking up into his face. "Wow, that looks horrible."

He gave a miserable grimace that was possibly an attempt at a smile. "At least I look as bad as I feel," he croaked, then went into another coughing fit.

"I'm so sorry," Nina said, getting to her feet.

"Apology accepted," Charlie said when he caught his breath again.

Nina chuckled. Even with his face on fire he still had a sense of humour.

"How about some milk in your tea this time? It might be soothing on your throat," she said. "I've got real milk, I picked some up in town. And an ice pack to keep it cold. Oh, hey, do you want some of the ice on your face, too?"

"Yes please," he mumbled through his swollen lips, lying back on the couch with the washcloth pressed over his face. "Both."

Nina wrapped some of the ice in a dish towel, put it in his hands, then went back into the kitchen to make the tea. What on earth could generate an allergic reaction this severe?

"Here you go," she said, taking the tea into the living room. Charlie was stretched out on the couch with the ice pack on his eyes. "Hey, come on, you'd better sit up to drink this." She got her arm under his shoulders and helped him up, taking the ice pack from between his fingers.

His eyes were swollen so badly he could barely open them, and his nose was still streaming. He groped around on the coffee table. "Did you say there is some Kleenex?"

"Just toilet paper," she said, putting it into his hands. He pulled a long length off the roll, wadded it up and blew his nose. "Ugh," he said. "Where's the ice?" He fished around in front of him. His hand fell on Nina's leg, and his whole body stilled. "Oh—not ice..." he said finally.

"No, it's not." Nina gently took his hand and moved it off her thigh. "Come on, buddy. You were going to have your tea, remember?" She put the handle of the cup between his fingers, then picked up his other hand and wrapped it around the mug. "There you go. See? Nice cuppa." She guided the cup to his mouth.

He had been passive at first, but now he resisted. "I can do it," he mumbled, his swollen lips trying to form into a smile. "I'm not that out of it." He took a careful sip. "Thanks, lady."

"There you go then. Have your tea like a good boy, and then get some more rest."

"Yes, Mummy," he said, obediently taking another sip of his tea.

Nina snorted. That hand on her thigh had not felt like he saw her in a maternal role, once he had figured out what he had gotten a hold of.

She went back to the kitchen and got a cup of tea for herself, then brought it into the living room. Charlie was stretched out on the couch again, taking up all of the space.

But there was no other place to sit. She parked her tea cup on the coffee table and moved over his work boots that he had shucked at the end of the couch—those things were heavy! Steel toes? Then she picked up his feet and shoved them up a bit. “Budge up, I want to sit down.” He moved his feet out of the way, and Nina plopped herself into the remaining corner of the couch, trying not to sit on his feet.

He was still wearing his holey sock, or else all of his socks had a hole in the exact same spot over the right big toe. Weird though that idea was, it had to be that, because if he had been wearing the same pair of socks for three days straight, they should have stunk out the whole room—and they didn’t, no more so than any guy’s feet did after a few hours of boot-wearing.

Nina settled back into the couch and picked up her tea with a sigh.

“Did you get your phone charge cable in town?” Charlie mumbled from under his cooling head pack.

“Yes,” Nina said, and swallowed hard as the shock about the disastrous email from June hit her in the solar plexus again. “I almost wish I hadn’t.”

“Why?”

“I lost my job.” Nina’s throat was trying to close up.

“What??” He took the ice pack from his face and sat up, trying to look at her from his swollen eyes.

“Yeah.” Nina tried to suppress a sniffle. “My boss emailed me. About a dozen times. She got mad because she couldn’t get a hold of me—because my phone was locked in the car—and so she fired me. By email. Which is just the sort of thing she would do, the wi—” Nina broke off.

"Witch," he completed. "That's a bugger."

"Yes, it is," Nina said. "Not that it was long in coming; she's like that."

"Sounds like you're well shot of that job then?"

"It was work," Nina said, "with a paycheque. Now I have to start over again. Go job hunting." She stared into her tea cup at the milky liquid. "I do have to live somehow."

Charlie laid back down again. "Where *do* you live? I mean, where's home?"

"Vancouver," Nina said, taking a sip from her tea. "I'm in an apartment in Burnaby."

"No family?"

"My mom is in Phoenix. She liked the snowbirding so well, she ended up staying there and married an American."

He reached for the roll of toilet paper with one hand, balanced the cold pack over his eyes so he didn't have to hold it, then pulled a length of tissue off the roll to wipe his nose. "Do you own your apartment?"

"Good gracious, no! Who could afford an apartment in Burnaby?"

"Is it expensive?"

"Uh, yeah? Greater Vancouver?"

He made some kind of motion that might have been a shrug. "I've never lived there," he said, wadding up his used nose rag and adding it to the growing pile of snotty toilet paper balls on the floor beside him.

"Well, unless I get a job quickly I won't be living there any longer either..." Nina said. "I guess I'll have to try to sell this place as quickly as I can and see what I can get for it."

"No!" He snatched the cold pack off his eyes and half sat up, then sank back again. "Sorry, none of my business."

Nina gave him a look, but of course, he couldn't see her with his cold pack over his eyes. "No, it's not, is it?" She took a sip from her tea. "What do you think I could get for this place? How much do properties go for around here?"

He shrugged again. "Not a clue."

"You must know what your own place is worth," Nina said. "Come to think of, where do you live? Do you have your own house?"

Charlie got shaken by a major coughing fit, but somehow it didn't sound nearly as bad as the others—in fact, rather like he was prolonging it on purpose. Now why would he do that?

"Do you want some more tea for your throat?" she asked him anyway.

"Yes, please," he said when he caught his breath.

When she came back from the kitchen with his tea, he was sitting up and had the photo album in his hands, trying to peer at it from his swollen eyes.

"That's Miranda!" he said, pointing at the first couple of pictures. He turned the pages and held out his other hand for the tea. "Thanks, love."

Nina handed him the cup. "You're welcome, but I'm not your lo—" Her eye fell on one of the pictures in the book. "What the heck??" She dropped down onto the couch next to Charlie and snatched the photo album from his hands. "That's—*that's my grandmother*!!"

The picture showed the two of them, the Miranda lady and Granny, on the back patio of the cottage, proudly smiling into the camera as they displayed two identical "wedding ring" quilts. Miranda looked much younger than in the other photos, and the weird washed out colours of the photo and its format—about three inches square, with a white edge around it—said it was from sometime in the sixties. Nina knew the other young woman was her grandmother; she had a photo of her from around the same time on her dresser at home. She was even wearing the same outfit—a striped sundress, and a big picture hat like Miranda's.

So Miranda had known Granny! That explained a thing or two—maybe?

Nina turned the page. More Miranda and vegetables (labelled "purple pole beans, tasty" or "blue hubbard, good yield" or "Boston bibb, very tender"), or Miranda and fruit ("Pink Lady and Jonagold apples, sweet"; "fall-bearing raspberries, prolific"; "red-stalked rhubarb, best for pies"; "Red Haven peaches, best for all-purpose"). Miranda with the blonde-moustached guy from the café (no labels on that one). Miranda standing on her front porch ("Purple clematis, grown from seed"; "coronation grapes and concords; Jelly '94"). Miranda...

"Hey, I recognize that one!" Charlie said, arresting Nina's hand as she was about to turn the page. It was the photo of Miranda in the back garden of the cottage, leaning on her hoe and smiling at the camera. "I took that one!"

"Say what?" Nina turned to look at him. The swelling in his eyes was starting to go down a bit and he could open his eyes wider. So he was actually looking at the picture.

"I'm serious," he said, "I took that snapshot. We were cleaning out the brambles in the corner of the garden, and Miranda was noodling around afterwards, doing a bit of hoeing and weeding. I found the camera in the house, and the colours were so lovely I took a picture of her and it."

"When was this?" Nina said, but Charlie started coughing again. Okay, that definitely sounded fake this time. "What is it with you and not answering questions?" she asked irritably.

Charlie stopped hacking abruptly, as if he had been caught in the act. "Uh, I, uh, don't remember." He reached across Nina's lap to the album and turned the page. "Is this the end of the book?"

Nina stared. There was Granny again, with Miranda. Nina recognized that outfit, too—it had been Granny's fancy-occasion dress, a sleeveless black gown with a loosely crocheted stole over top. Miranda seemed kind of dressed up, too, in some kind of tiered gypsy skirt and a peasant blouse that looked like something from the early eighties. But what really got Nina was the setting, and who they were with. Between them stood a man in a white cassock with wide sleeves, a scarlet surplice over top and an embroidered stole draped around his neck, the three of them silhouetted against a multi-coloured stained-glass window as they stood around what clearly was a baptismal font in a church. In Miranda's arms was what at first glance looked like a bundle of clothes—white, frilly, lacy clothes, until you noticed the round bump on one end that was covered with a lacy, frilly bonnet. A baby.

And not just any baby.

"Virginia Marie, September 18th, 1994," it said underneath the photo.

Virginia Marie? Nina. Nina herself.

And Miranda was her godmother.

"Did you know this?" Nina held out the photo album accusingly.

"Know what, darling?"

Nina was too upset to bother, so she let the "darling" slide. "This!" She stabbed her finger at the caption of the photo. "That Miranda is—is—That that's me!"

He peered at the picture from his swollen eyes. "Oh. That's you, is it? Hmm. That does put another spin on things, doesn't it."

"But I never knew anything about this! Nobody ever said anything!" She'd had a godmother. And had no idea about it. She was getting very, very fed up with having things just happen to her without getting a choice in the matter.

Charlie put his hand on Nina's shoulder. "I'm sorry," he said.

"Didn't Miranda ever, I dunno, say something?"

"No, I can't say she did," Charlie said. "But it was a lo—Uh, no, she did not say anything about a goddaughter."

Nina ran her fingers over the picture. "I would have been three months old," she said.

Charlie made a strange huffing noise, then abruptly changed the subject. "I'm getting hungry," he said. "Did you say you bought groceries?"

Evening and a Bottle of Wine

Nina hadn't had such a comfortable evening in a long time. They cracked that bottle of wine Charlie had brought the day before, and then he showed her how to make a mini-fire in the fireplace so they could make toast. It was too warm to make a real fire, and even so they had to have the patio door and the window open to get a bit of a breeze moving through the room, but it felt like sitting around a campfire.

It gradually started to get dark outside, the trees out back silhouetted against the darkening sky, and a chorus of crickets made itself heard through the open doors.

"We could use some light," Charlie said, and he got up to take down one of the candles that were sitting on the mantelpiece. He fished around on the lintel. "Where are the matches?"

"They should be right up there," Nina said. "Or, no, we used them for the fire."

"Ah, never mind," Charlie said. "We can light it on the fire." He held out the candle to the flame, but apparently with his swollen eyes he couldn't see properly what he was doing and stuck it in too far so it started to melt.

"Ack, no, what the heck are you doing?" Nina took the candle out of his hand. "I don't have candles to just burn up for nothing, you know!"

He pouted at her. "You don't trust me!"

Nina laughed. "No, I don't," she said. "Let me do that." She lit the first candle on the fire, then used it to put the flame to the second one. A wax drop fell down from the candle and splattered on the page of photo album. Nina yelped.

"What?" said Charlie, who was leaning back on the couch, his damp cloth over his eyes. He took it off his face and sat up. "Did you mess things up?"

"Kind of," Nina said. "Dripped some wax on the album."

"Well, my dear woman—"

"I'm *not* your dear woman!"

"—my dear woman—"

Nina glared at him, but he pretended not to see.

"—you don't light one candle from the other by bringing the *lit* one to the *unlit* one. Or you get exactly what—well, what you got. Always, always bring the unlit candle to the lit one, that's the proper way to do it." He leaned back against the cushion and laid the damp cloth over his eyes again, a smile playing around the corners of his mouth.

"Yadda yadda yadda!" Nina said. "Mr. Know-it-all. If I had let you do it, you would have melted the whole entire candle in the fire like it was a marshmallow. So stop lecturing me." She blew a raspberry.

"Well, darling..." he began, the smile on his mouth getting broader.

"Do—not—'darling'—me!" Nina said, smacking him on the arm with each word.

He sat up and caught her hand, the washcloth dropping on his lap. "Now, now, darling!"

Nina growled at him.

Charlie laughed. "I'll try to stop," he said. "It's a habit I brought from the old country. At least I haven't called you 'ducky' yet."

Nina shuddered theatrically. "Now *that* would get you a one-way ticket out the door, *darling*."

Charlie sat up straight and saluted with the washcloth. "Yes, ma'am! I shall endeavour to control my impulses, ma'am!"

"Good," Nina said, reaching for the album and running her finger over the spot where the wax had landed. "I'll hold you to it."

"Did you get the wax on the picture?" Charlie asked, leaning back against the cushions again with his washcloth.

"No, thank goodness," Nina said, picking at the wax droplet with her fingernail. "It landed right beside it. Hah, it's covering up the first part of 'Virginia'—just as well."

"So, speaking of Virginia," Charlie said, "did you read *Orlando* yet?"

"No, I haven't read O*rlando* yet," Nina said. "Planning to, though. I was too busy with re-reading *Pride and Prejudice.*"

"Ah, yes! 'It is a truth universally acknowledged that a single man in possession of a large fortune must be in a want of a wife...'"

"You have read it?"

"Don't sound so surprised," he said, raising the cloth from his face. "It's a classic."

"Not one guys are usually into."

"Now who is being prejudiced?"

"Or who is being proud, for that matter?"

"Touché," he said, getting comfortable again. "Hey, is there any more wine?"

Nina poured him another glass, took his hand and put the glass into it. "That's a pretty nice wine," she said.

"No kidding," he said, taking an appreciative sip, holding the cloth over his eyes with his other hand. "What's it called again?"

"What do you mean, what's it called? You were the one who brought it."

"Yes... well, I sort of just grabbed it."

"From the liquor store, you mean?"

He cleared his throat. "Uh, yeah, something like that." He took another sip.

Nina studied the bottle. "It's called 'Latitude Fifty'," she said. "From Gray Monk Winery in Lake Country."

"Lake Country?"

"Yeah, I think it's between Kelowna and Vernon."

"Ah. I thought that was called Winfield. Maybe they've renamed it. I seem to remember a number of lakes around there."

"Maybe? I don't know, I've not been there."

"It's a nice area," he said. "Worth a visit."

"Mm-hm," Nina said quietly, taking a sip of her own wine and staring at the fire in the fireplace. She was starting to feel decidedly mellow.

"So," Charlie said after a longish, comfortable silence in which only the crickets were talking, "you've been reading Jane Austen, but not Virginia Woolf. What else is on that book shelf?"

"Hmm?" Nina turned her head and realized she was leaning against Charlie's arm. Oh. She sat up again. "Umm, books. On shelf." She put the wine glass on the coffee table. "There's Grimm's Fairy Tales!"

"Oh yes. Not nearly as grim as they're made out to be. Will you read me a story?"

"Don't feel like it," Nina said. She picked up the wine bottle. "Do you want a bit more?"

"More what?"

"Latitititude Fifty," Nina said. "There's enough for a tiny bit more each."

He laughed and held out his glass. "All right then, bring it on."

Nina divided up the wine, put down the bottle and leaned back against the couch. This was comfortable... No sound but the chirping of the crickets, the little cracks and crackles of the fire, and the beat of Charlie's heart. Charlie's heart? Oh. She seemed to be leaned right up against his shoulder, with her ear pressed to his chest, and he had his arm around her. Quite cozy, this. His flannel shirt was nice and soft...

She turned her head into his shoulder. His beard was just a bit scratchy on her forehead. "You should probably go home soon," she said drowsily, not making a move to shift so he could get up.

"Do I have to?" he replied in the same tone, tucking his arm more closely around her.

"Nah, not really," she said. "You could sleep on the couch."

"Aww, the couch?"

Nina gave him a weak slap on the leg—more of a pat, really. "Don't get ideas, dude."

"Too late, darling, I've already got them." His voice was a warm rumble through his chest.

"Hmph. You're still calling me darling."

"I know, darling." His fingers were playing with Nina's hair, and it felt rather nice.

"You promised to stop," she said, leaning her cheek into his caressing hand.

"I did, didn't I? I'm so sorry, luv, won't happen again."

Nina huffed softly. "There, I could kick you out for not listening to me."

"Sure, but you wouldn't, would you? A poor wounded man?"

"Oh yeah, poor baby."

They fell silent for a while again, listening to the cricket chorus. Then a frog joined in.

Ribbet, ribbet!

Croooooak! Crooooak!

Ribbet, ribbet!

Crooooak!

"What's that sound?" Nina asked sleepily.

"It's a frog."

"No, the other sound!"

"Which one?"

"The loud 'croooak.'"

"Like I said, it's a frog."

"No, they make that 'ribbet ribbet' sound, not a 'cr oooak.'"

"Some do."

"I've never heard one do that before."

"Well, now you have," Charlie said. "The 'ribbet' frogs are only in America; in Europe, all frogs croak."

"Mhm," Nina said. "Do they." She thought for a bit. "So the Frog Prince must have croaked? That's like, in *Shrek 2*, where the father changes back into the frog, and Donkey says 'He's croaked!' Or is that Puss in Boots who says it?"

His soft chuckle rumbled through his chest. "I haven't got the faintest idea what you are talking about." His voice was getting slow and sleepy.

"Oh, you know. The *Shrek* movies. The second one, where Shrek and Fiona visit her parents."

"'Fraid not," he said. "Doesn't ring a bell."

"Hm," said Nina. "What planet have you lived on the last twenty years?"

His thumb stroked the side of her face. "What indeed..." he murmured softly.

"I always liked the Frog Prince, the story, I mean, not the dude," Nina said. "Although I don't know if I would have kissed him."

"You could always go with the original Grimm's version," Charlie said. "Chuck him against the wall."

"Sounds violent."

"Yes... I think kissing is preferable. Want to try it?" Nina could feel that he turned his face towards her.

"Hah, you wish," she said.

"Sure do."

"Don't push it."

He settled back against the cushions with a slight sigh. "Well, you cannot blame a man for trying, sweetheart."

"Don't tell me what I can or cannot do," Nina said. "And don't call me sweetheart."

"Sorry, dear."

Nina turned her head and looked up at his face. "You're bad, you know that?"

His still-swollen eyes were closed, and his head leaned back against the back rest of the couch. "So they tell me," he murmured, "so they tell me."

Nina became aware of a certain pressure in her bladder region.

"I gotta go to the can," she said, making no move to get up.

"Then you had better go."

"I'd better." Still no move.

At least five minutes went by.

Nina woke up again.

"I was going to go to the bathroom, wasn't I," she mumbled sleepily.

"So you said." He stirred and moved his arm.

"I think I should probably go to bed," Nina said, and with an effort made herself sit up straight.

"Mm-hm," Charlie said, his hand sliding down her back and resting for a moment in the middle, warm and comfortable.

With a groan, Nina hoisted herself up from the couch, and her mouth cracked open in a yawn. "Okay, I gotta get. Do you need a pillow and blanket?"

"If you have some to spare... But I'm fine like this, too."

"All rightie then. I'll go look. G'night, Charlie."

"Night, Nina. Thank you for letting me stay."

"It's okay. Sleep tight, 'kay?"

"You too," he said, and as Nina turned away, she heard him very softly add, "my darling."

Dead Battery

The bright morning sunlight fell on the note that lay in the middle of the coffee table.

"Dear Nina," it said in small, slanted printing, the points of the N stabbing into the next line of the writing, *"I'm so very sorry. Believe me, if I could help it, I would. Thank you so much for the place to stay and the lovely evening. Until next time, C."*

Of the guy himself, not a hair was in sight. Not even his snotty nose rags.

Nina dropped onto the couch and let her hands with the paper sink to her lap. She stared out the window. Gone again. And the patio door was firmly locked, as was—she got up to check—the front door. Did Charlie have a front door key? But then why did he never let himself in? No, he couldn't have a key. So how had he let himself out of a locked room?

Nina huffed and got to her feet. She might as well get some breakfast. She wandered into the kitchen and found the washed wine glasses on the drain board by the sink; the empty wine bottle stood in the corner of the cupboard. So at least that had been real. And it looked like Charlie had been nice enough to do the dishes before he legged it. Good for him. Nina sniffed.

She put on the kettle and took the jar of instant coffee from the IGA bag. At least she could have some java to start the day. A day in which she would have to decide what to do with her future. Job gone down the drain—now what? Her saved buffer money wouldn't go very far to pay rent on the apartment in Burnaby. She would have to give notice. There were still a couple of weeks to the end of the month, and she was paid up until then; so enough time to find something else.

Actually, the very first thing she had to do was to get back to Vancouver and retrieve her stuff from the office before June consigned it to the dumpster. Nina wouldn't put it past her to do just that; June was "nice" that way. And there was Granny's paperweight, solid glass with a couple of blue marbled swirls inside it—it would break Nina's heart to lose it. So, back in the car it was, and down to the Big Smoke.

Nina felt almost reluctant. She was starting to get used to the quiet and clean air of the country. Well, she would have to come back really soon anyway, in order to put the sale of the cottage into motion. Really soon.

She fished yesterday's cinnamon bun out of its paper bag, popped the lid off the little plastic container with the icing, and got a knife to put the icing on. One big bite—the cinnamon bun had gotten a little dry, but it was still good. Delicious, in fact. That bakery, whatever it was called, was another reason to come back to this place—Koffee and Krumble, that was it. She'd not had a chance to try out their other goodies; there had been a superb-looking cheesecake, and the carrot cake looked scrumptious, too. And there was a coconut-apricot square, and some kind of walnut thing or whatever that was, all of which looked fantastic. Plus, something about that Ye Olde Worlde atmosphere of the place appealed to Nina. Including the black and white photos on the wall—the retro black and white photos. Nina wondered how many of them had been colour pictures to start with, like those of Miranda.

Yes, Miranda. Nina still couldn't believe it that she actually was—or had been—her godmother. She hadn't even known she *had* a godmother, that she had ever been christened. But apparently she had, by Granny's doing. So, at least that explained to a small extent why Miranda had left her the house. She had certainly never done anything else that was godmotherly—never even a birthday card.

It was interesting that Granny had never said anything about Miranda, either. But then, maybe she had? Granny hadn't been very voluble at the best of times—there were a lot of things about her and about her life that Nina had no clue about, and would never get a clue about now, either. But Granny *did* tell Nina stories. And especially the one about The Garden of Good Things. It had been Nina's favourite.

She leaned her hands on the edge of the sink, staring out through the window into the tangled garden beyond. There was a garden, Granny said... once upon a time... full of carrots and pumpkins and tomatoes and strawberries and lettuces and apples and peas—and flowers you could eat... "You can eat that, you know," Charlie's voice echoed in Nina's memory, "it tastes like cucumber..." And then, Granny's voice continued, a little girl walked into the garden... and she found treasure. Or fairies. Or talking animals. Once, there had even been a prince... "Do you want to try a kiss?" said Charlie's voice in Nina's mind....

But Nina had not cared for the prince in Granny's story—she had only been eight, and at that age boys have cooties—so he became a talking squirrel instead, which she liked much better.

The bushes outside the window rustled, and the chipmunk skittered up one of the branches and down another. He stopped, turned his head with a quick darting motion, and looked at Nina through the window. For a full five seconds they stared at each other, not blinking, then with a twitch of his tail the chipmunk was gone.

Nina shook herself. Yeah, right. Talking chipmunks, sleeping princes, enchanted gardens—what next? They were flippin' *stories*, fairy tales, not twenty-first century realities. She was no longer eight years old; boys didn't have cooties—at least not most of them—and there was no such thing as an enchanted garden. A messy garden, maybe, but that's as far as it went. A garden that needed weeding quite badly to find all those amazing fruits and vegetables that were still there in spite of having been left neglected for, what—twenty-five years? It had to be that long, if Miranda had last been heard of sometime in the nineties.

But then, why had the house been so clean? *Did* Charlie have a key, had he been looking after the place? If he did have a key, she would have to get it off him when she found a buyer.

But first, go to Vancouver and get her stuff. Then talk to her landlady about cancelling the lease of the apartment.

Or maybe—maybe June had cooled off by now and would let Nina keep her job?

The thought left a bad taste in Nina's mouth. She was tired of June, tired of the job, tired of having to drag herself down to the office every day, tired of being at the mercy of June's petty tyranny.

She walked into the bedroom, hauled her clothes out of the dresser drawer she had put them in, tossed them into her suitcase, zipped it shut, and picked up her purse.

At the front door, she paused. If Charlie did have a key, maybe he'd want to know what happened to her... She got a pen from her purse, took the note he had left for her, and turned it over.

"Charlie," she wrote, *"Going to Vancouver to deal with stuff; be back soon to put house on market."* She paused. How to sign it? "Yours, Nina"? "See you soon, Nina"? "Take care, Nina"? "Love, Nina"? No, definitely not that. In the end, she just went with *"Nina."* She put the note prominently on the coffee table box, weighed it down with the empty wine bottle—time to recycle that when she got back—and made her way out to the car.

She unlocked it, stuck her suitcase in the back, tossed her purse on the passenger seat, and slid behind the wheel.

There was her phone on the dash, still plugged into the 12-Volt outlet.

"Oh no!" She grabbed the phone and frantically pushed the start button. The screen lit up with the lock symbol, and Nina heaved a sigh of relief. The phone hadn't drained again. She drew her finger across the screen, connecting the dots in the checkmark shape that was her lock pattern, and there was the West Coast beach that was her wallpaper. Now to get out of here. She booted up Google Maps, punched in the address of her apartment, then hit "Directions." She should get there in 6 hours and 23 minutes, the app figured. All right, fair enough.

Nina put the key in the ignition and turned it. Nothing happened.

What?

She tried it again.

Nothing. Total silence from the engine, no lights appearing on the dashboard, nothing.

The phone had drained the battery completely.

Nina hit her forehead against the steering wheel. "I. Don't. Believe. This!" she said, thumping with each word. "Why—why—why—WHY?? This. Is. Ridiculous!!" She never did that sort of thing in Vancouver, ever. Not often, anyway. Only once in the last five years or so. But here, it happened over and over. Almost as if something didn't want her to leave.

Well, at least she had a working phone, *with* cell connection. And her wallet, with a BCAA card. With a sigh that came right from her toes, she reached for her purse.

Twenty minutes later, she was back in the house, her feet up on the coffee table box, waiting for the tow truck so she could get a jump start. "We have longer than usual wait times; thank you for your patience," the BCAA machine had told her in between its indeterminable clips of elevator music—the same tune over and over and over, until Nina was ready to scream. When she finally got someone on the phone, they promised to send a tow truck out to her as soon as possible. "Could be a while, though," said the BCAA lady on the phone. "I had a call-out not too long ago from that town, and the client called back three times to check if they had been forgotten."

So here Nina sat, with her feet up on the coffee table box and the fat copy of Grimm's *Children's and Household Tales* in her hand, waiting. For the first little while, she kept turning on her phone to check the time—surely they would come soon? But then she realized that what she was doing was draining the battery, and it wouldn't make the BCAA truck come any faster. And surely, if they were late they would give her a call? She had left them a number.

One more time she turned on the phone. There was a signal, right? Actually, no, there wasn't. What a pain. Nina took the phone and stepped out onto the terrace. Voíla, cell signal! She turned back into the room—the signal dropped. Back out, signal, immediately inside the French doors, gone. She walked across the room and stepped out through the front door. Nope. Maybe it was the roof that was doing it? Nina walked down the three steps from the porch, and sure enough, there was the signal. So she had no cell signal as long as she was in the house. What a nuisance.

However, looking at her missed calls, there wasn't one from the last half hour, so it looked like the BCAA guy was plain old late. She stuck her phone into her pocket and went back into the house. She would just have to periodically step back outside to check if there was a call.

There wasn't.

An hour later, Nina had read "Hansel and Gretel," "Snow White and Rose Red," "Little Briar Rose," "Little Brother and Little Sister," and "The Goose Girl," and between each story had checked for phone calls. Nothing. Should she call BCAA and complain? But that would require going outside again and waiting around, which was more tedious than waiting inside. Besides, outside, there was the bear...

She became aware of a noise intruding on her conscience.

"Hello? Hey, hi, anybody there?" came a faint voice from outside. Charlie? Was he back?

Nina sat up and looked out the French doors. No, no Charlie there. She noticed a slight feeling of disappointment, and she tucked the discovery of it away in a back corner of her mind. No time for thinking about her feelings at the moment.

"Hey, hello!" the voice was still calling. Nina turned around to look out the front window. There in the tangled front yard stood a man, with a scraggly dirty blond ponytail under a baseball cap. It was Jerry the bookstore guy! Why was he here? And what the heck was he *doing*?

As Nina watched, Jerry went up to the steps of the porch, lifting his foot to mount the stairs. But it was as if the porch was shucking him off. When Nina was a kid, she had had some super-strong, thick bar magnets. What happened to Jerry looked like what happened when you tried to push the two north poles of the magnets together: they repelled one another, the one slipping sideways past the other. Jerry seemed to hit an invisible air cushion that made it impossible for him to even get his foot on the bottom step, it kept slipping sideways. He gave up, stepped back and yelled again.

"Yo, is anyone home?"

Nina pulled open the front door. "Hi! What can I do for you?"

The guy looked up and did a double-take.

"Oh, hi, it's you," he said. "Aren't you the lady that was asking about Miranda McManus at the store yesterday?"

"Yes, I am."

He took off his baseball cap and scratched his head. "Why were you asking about her when you're living in her house?"

Nina shrugged. "Because I don't know much about her," she said. "But what are you doing here?"

He put his baseball cap back on. "You called BCAA—or someone did, anyway, about that green Toyota out there?"

"Yes, that would be me." Why was a bookstore guy answering BCAA calls?

"I brought the tow truck," he said, jerking his thumb over his shoulder in the direction of the street. "It's my brother's, but he's in bed with a bad back, so I'm filling in."

"Oh, I see! Well, come on up on the porch; I'll grab my keys. Oh, wait—" Nina had remembered that Jerry seemed to have this weird disability when it came to stair climbing. But then the guy lifted his foot, carefully, and placed it on the bottom stair—and with two steps, he was up on the porch. Huh, interesting.

"So what is it you need done?" Jerry asked when they got out to the car.

"My battery died," Nina said. "I left my phone plugged into the cigarette lighter."

"Ah," he said. "Need a jump then?"

"Yes, I figure."

"Ah," he said again. He kept looking down the street, in the direction of the driveway of the pink house.

"That's Jadice's house down there," he said wistfully.

"Well, I'm not going down there myself anymore," Nina said. "There's a bear living around there. I tried twice to get to the house, to see if someone was there and I could get help, and each time only just got away without being eaten."

His head flew around. "A bear?? What's it doing there? I mean, did it make its den there or something?"

"No idea. Like I said, I got out of there as quickly as I could, I wasn't going to hang around and play twenty questions with it."

"But, I mean, Jadice's house—you can't let a bear get in there! It could make a huge mess of it!"

"Maybe *you* can't," Nina said, getting a little impatient with him, "but I'm not going back there, and I don't really care other than that I don't like having a bear this close in the neighbourhood."

"You're right!" he said, pulling back his shoulders. "I am going to take care of that. Jadice had a beautiful house, she really cared about it. It would break her heart if it was wrecked when she comes back."

"Is she coming back?" Nina asked. She didn't really care though. She reached into her car and popped the hood.

"Well, why not?" he said, sounding defensive. "It's a nice place here." Apparently Nina's pointed look finally penetrated, and he pulled open the door of the tow truck cab, climbed in and manoeuvred the vehicle into place.

He had Nina's car jumpstarted in fairly short order.

"Okay, here it is," he said, dropping the Toyota's hood into place.

"Thanks," Nina said. "Could you stick around for a few minutes while I get the house locked up? I was leaving for Vancouver, and I don't want the car to die again before I go."

"Yeah, sure," he said. "I have to get back to the store, but I can hang on a couple minutes. Just don't take too long."

Nina collected her things, went to the bathroom, then closed and locked up the door behind her. She felt a little sad at the thought of selling this place—she was starting to get attached to it.

Jerry hadn't seen her yet. He sat in the cab of the idling tow truck, pointing his cell phone camera at the side of the street where Jadice's house was, then taking it down and tapping at the screen. Probably adding the photo to his file of stalker photos of Jadice.

Nina looked over in the same direction. You couldn't really see Jadice's house, the trees were way too dense, with thick shrubs between them. One shook, and for a brief second, Nina thought she saw a black shape. It stopped, and Nina felt that someone was looking straight at her. Her heart jumped into her mouth, and she gave a gasp. But then it was gone, and all there was in that spot was shrubbery. Had it really been...

Jerry climbed out of the cab of the truck. "Okay, you all set then? If you keep the car running for a while, the battery should re-charge; just don't turn it off for at least an hour."

"Yes, thanks," Nina said. "I appreciate the help."

"Yeah," he said. "Thanks for the heads up about the bear; I know exactly what to do about that. My brother's got a gun," he added ominously.

Nina wasn't really listening. She was wondering if she could make it to the coast in time to get Granny's paperweight from the office tonight. And where had she put her landlady's contact information?

She got in the car, shifted into reverse, and backed out onto the road. One more shift into first, and she was on her way back to the city. Seven hours should get her there; she hoped that she would make it over the mountains before dark.

Return to Houghton

A week later, Nina felt a curious sense of homecoming as she pulled into Houghton. The crate full of her stuff that sat on the passenger's seat was rattling gently as she angle-parked the car in front of Koffee and Krumble. She wanted a cinnamon bun before heading out to the cottage and a nice latte of some kind, as she couldn't use her espresso machine in the cottage. She had her French press coffee maker with her—it only required boiling water, so no plug like the electric coffee machine. But it still wasn't as quick and easy as the latter. She had also brought every battery-operated light she could lay hands on, including an LED camping lantern that was astonishingly bright. So, light, and proper coffee, as well as another couple of ice packs which she intended to buy at the gas station—she should be able to hold out for a while in the cottage, depending on how long it would take to get the place set up for selling it.

And sell it she must, sadly. There was no way she could afford to keep a holiday cottage in the backwoods of BC. She had to work to live, and work—at least the kind she was qualified for—was only to be had in the city.

But first, cinnamon buns and coffee. Maybe the coffee shop people could point her in the direction of a realtor, too. Or better yet, she'd ask Jerry at the bookstore; he knew the town.

Nina pulled at the door handle of Once Upon a Tyme Pre-Read Books, but the door wouldn't budge. She peered through the glass panel. There was light on inside, but no sign of the owner. Hmph.

Oh well, there was always the coffee shop entrance to the bookstore. Nina pulled open the door, releasing an aroma of fresh-ground coffee, warm cinnamon buns, and spice cookies. She sniffed appreciatively.

"Oh hey," the young barista said, "you're still in town?"

"Again," Nina said. "I had to go back to Vancouver for something. I'm probably only here for a few days this time, depends on how quickly I can get the cottage on the market. Can I get a triple venti caramel macchiato and a couple of cinnamon buns? One of them to go, the rest for here."

"Okey dokey," the girl said cheerfully. "So you're not going to stay in town then? Yeah, I get that. Would be nice to have a house here to come back to, though, wouldn't it."

"Yes, it would," Nina replied, surprising herself by the fervour with which she said it. Two weeks ago she hadn't known this place existed... "But unfortunately, I can't afford it. So, is there such a thing as a real estate agency around here?"

"There's a Royal LePage office behind the drugstore," the girl said, carefully swirling foam on top of Nina's mug of coffee. "I think it's only Sue Hammond who runs it, but you could check it out." She took a squeeze bottle with a skinny tip and drizzled caramel on top of the foam in a zigzag pattern, then picked up a skewer and drew it through the drizzle in the other direction, making a weave pattern out of the golden brown lines. "Okay, one triple venti caramel macchiato for here, and coming up is one Cindy's cinnamon swirl delight for here and one to go. That's eleven eighty."

Nina pulled out her wallet. She would have to get more conservative with her spending habits; almost twelve bucks for a coffee and a couple of pastries was too much for her now non-existent budget. Who knew when she'd next see a paycheque once the last one from June had cleared—always hoping that June would actually pay her. Nina didn't fancy having to go to small claims court for it.

"Well, thanks for the info about the realtor," she said. "I was going to ask Jerry from the bookstore, but the door is locked."

"Yeah, he's not there. I'm keeping an eye on the bookstore for him. It's not like there's a ton of people coming in there anyway; you're the first one who has asked all afternoon."

"Is he out doing another tow truck run for his brother? He gave me a jump start when I was leaving and had run my battery dry with charging my phone."

"Oops!" The girl giggled. "I hate it when that happens. Joe's had to bail out my mom a couple of times, too. My dad gets really mad at her when she forgets to turn off the car lights or whatever and he has to come get her, so she got BCAA—that way she can call the tow truck and Dad never finds out about it. But actually, no, Jerry isn't doing a tow truck run—Joe's back doing it himself. I guess his back got better." She put a plate with a warm cinnamon bun on the counter in front of Nina. "Oh, wait, you like extra icing, right?" She took the icing bag and gave the bun another swirl of the gooey white frosting. "And I won't warm up the to-go one, right? It'll go dry otherwise."

"Thanks, I appreciate that," Nina said, picking up her plate. "By the way, I don't think I ever got your name?"

"It's Caleigh," the girl said.

"Mine's Nina."

The girl smiled at her. "Nice to meetcha, Nina." She slid one of the golden pinwheels into a brown paper bag, added a plastic container with icing, and folded over the top of the bag. "So, yeah, Jerry's off on a bit of a bender," she said. "Practically every day he hares off somewhere with Joe's gun. Cindy keeps telling him that if the conservation officers get a hold of him he could be in trouble; he hasn't even got a bear tag."

Nina looked up. "Bear tag?"

"Yeah, he's after a bear he says is running wild in the woods out there, by some kind of house. From what I understand, nobody lives there anymore, but he's obsessed about getting the bear away from there. Cindy said he had the hots for the lady who lived there or something." She giggled. "You didn't hear that from me though."

Oh no. Jerry loose with a gun, after a bear, *by her house.*

Nina put her plate and her cup back down on the counter. "Umm, Caleigh," she said quickly, "really sorry about that, but could I get those to go after all?"

Caleigh raised her eyebrows. "Oh, sure, if that's what you want. Do you want the cinnamon delight in a clamshell box? If I put it in a paper bag, the icing is going to stick to it."

"Uh—yeah, sure." Whatever, as long as it was quick...

She rushed out of the shop, awkwardly clutching the bag with the cold cinnamon bun between the fingers of the hand that balanced the coffee cup on top of the cardboard container that held the warm pastry and fishing for her car keys in her jeans pocket with the other hand. There was the key; now park the latte on the roof of the car, unlock the door, plop the takeout container on the dash, slide into the driver's seat—wait, the coffee! She ducked back out, grabbed the coffee, and got back into her seat. She put the key in the ignition, stepped on the clutch, started the engine, and took a sip from her latte at the same time.

Yow! That was hot! She sucked air over her scalded lip and deposited the coffee cup in the car's cup holder.

Twelve bucks worth of snacks, and she wasn't even taking time to appreciate them properly... But she couldn't sit and savour her coffee. She had to get back to the cottage to make sure there wasn't—wasn't *something* going weird. Not that she would be sad to hear the bear was taken care of and she didn't have to worry about getting eaten in her own neighbourhood, but somehow, a guy with a gun—it wasn't right.

Nina didn't even need Google Maps to know where she was going—the turnoff to Hawthorn Lane seemed as if it had a spotlight on it. She rattled over the dirt road, clutching the steering wheel, came to a stop with a spattering of gravel, and killed the engine. She jumped out of the car, listened, then looked along the road. There was no other car in sight, nothing parked by the side of the road, and all was quiet—well, forest-quiet, anyway, with birds chirping, small creatures rustling through the underbrush, an airplane going by far overhead...

Maybe she'd gotten hold of the wrong end of the stick and panicked for nothing. She calmed down a little. It was kind of weird anyway for her to have rushed out here because of a bookstore/tow truck guy who liked playing with guns.

She went around the car to the passenger side, ducked down, took the coffee out of the cup holder, then put her cinnamon buns on top of her crate of stuff, scooped it all up, and made her way through the gate in the hedge into the house.

The note on the coffee table hadn't moved. A little stab of disappointment hit Nina's heart. So he didn't have a key after all. Or at least he had not come in while she was gone. Ah well. It was not like she wanted some man coming into her house, making free of the place, while she was not at home, was it?

Nina parked her crate and cup on the coffee table, took the cinnamon buns from the top, put them aside, and extracted a small cubical box from the crate. She opened the top flap, took out a layer of tissue paper, and lifted out the glass paperweight with the blue swirls inside. Granny's glass paperweight. She carefully positioned it in the middle of the mantelpiece. She might not be here for long, but for that little while, she would make it home.

She had stepped back three paces to check its placement when a shot exploded right next to the house.

Shot

What the hell? Nina whirled around, yanked open the French doors and ran out onto the patio. What was going on?

Another crack of a shot—then a loud roar, crashing and thumping in the bushes towards the pink house.

And a third shot, another roar—that sounded like the bear. And it was closer to Nina's house than before.

Nina spun around to run back inside and slam the door behind her—an injured bear this close to her? She wasn't going to stick around for that!—when she heard the cry.

"Help!"

Nina stopped in her tracks. What... Had the bear got Jerry? But this didn't sound like somebody struggling with an animal, and there was no more growling—just a groan now, a human groan... "Help me... Nina..."

Charlie!!

And the sound was coming from close to the house—where was he?

Nina shoved through the black currant bushes around the patio, her heart racing. "Charlie?" She pushed aside tangled grass, woolly-looking tall spikes of yellow flowers, branches of bushes... "Charlie! Where are you?"

She reared back with a scream. There by the gap in the hedge lay the bear, hunched over; a low growling noise coming from his throat. He tried to rise on all fours, dragged himself a step forward—Nina backed up, step by step—her foot tangled in the long grass—she turned to look behind her.

"Nina, help me..."

Her head flew around. There was Charlie on the ground, where the bear had been a second earlier—where was the bear?

Charlie was hunched into himself, clutching his arm, blood running through his fingers, his face deadly white.

With three strides, Nina was at his side.

"Charlie! What the hell—what happened?"

He groaned. "Shot—gun shot..."

"Oh shit, shit, shit—I knew something like this was going to happen! That damn idiot with his gun! But where did the bear go? We need to get you out of here!" Nina frantically clapped her hands to her jeans pockets—her phone, where was her phone? She had to call 911—where was the thing? Not in the back pockets, not in the front—oh shit, it was safely in her purse, in the cottage—oh God... She dropped to her knees beside Charlie.

"Charlie, sweetheart—where are you hurt? Can you get up? Come on, try to get up—we need to get in the house! The bear is still around, it's going to come back—come on, please..."

He looked up at her, his blue eyes glazed with pain. "No ... bear ..." he groaned. Then he winked out of existence.

Nina gave a shout of surprise, and he was there again.

"What the..." Nina gasped, "Charlie!"

He gave a moan, then his eyes rolled back in his head and he went slack, his eyes closed and his head drooping back.

"Charlie, no!!" Nina grasped him by the shoulders. "Charlie, come on!"

His flannel jacket was damp with sweat, his muscles solid under her hands—and then they weren't, her hands grasping empty air—and then they were there again, hard and substantial—and once again he flickered out of existence and back into it.

Nina snatched her hands away like she had been burned, and her breath caught in a sob. "What's going on here? What's happening? Charlie..."

One more time he flickered away, like a flame in a fire; then for a split second on the ground in front of Nina was the bear, slack and still.

She jumped to her feet and stumbled back, but the animal had already winked out of existence again, and in its place lay Charlie, now completely still, his face a deathly greyish white.

Nina held her breath, staring at him. What was happening—the bear, Charlie, his disappearance—what was going on?

She realized that he wasn't moving at all. Nothing. Not only was he no longer disappearing and reappearing, he lay motionless, completely inert, not even his chest rising and falling the slightest bit with breathing.

Nina fell to her knees beside him. "No, Charlie! No no no no no! You can't be dead, please don't be dead, you can't! Come on!" Her breath came in gasping sobs as she frantically ran her hands over his rib cage, searching for a heart beat—it was supposed to be on the left side, wasn't it? But there was no movement, nothing—he felt dead under her fingers.

"Charlie, please, come on, please please please! Come *on*!" She pushed down on his rib cage with both her hands, the way she had seen in who-knew-how-many TV shows—vague memories of CPR lessons in high school gym class—come on, come *on*! If only she knew what to do! Artificial respiration, pumping the chest—it wasn't helping, nothing was happening... "Please, Charlie, please!"

Wait—what about mouth-to-mouth resuscitation? She really had no idea what she was doing, but you were supposed to plug their nose, she thought, and gently blow air inside their mouth until they started breathing on their own—weren't you?

Nina gave another sob. Then she drew in a deep breath, pinched Charlie's nose with one hand, grasped his chin with the other, opened his mouth, leaned down and placed her lips over his.

Please, Charlie, please, she begged him silently as she released her breath into him, please breathe! You have to live, come on, please! Breathe!

She took in another lungful of air to blow into him—and his eyes opened, he drew in a breath. Nina jerked back, letting go of his nose and chin, and stared at him. Was he really…?

One breath—another—and another—lung-filling sighs, as if he was waking from a deep sleep.

He looked around, and then his eyes found hers; he gazed up at her, his vision perfectly clear, his look conscious. A smile curved up the corner of his mouth.

"Nina," he said, "my darling," and his voice had its old, cheerful, caressing tone.

Nina gasped in a sob.

"You—you—you're alive!"

"Thanks to you, my darling." He reached out his hand. "That was a real Kiss of Life. Thank you."

Nina clasped his hand. "I—I thought—thought you were gone…"

"I believe I was," he said, his expression getting serious. "But your kiss brought me back."

"That—that wasn't a—a kiss!" Nina protested half-heartedly, her voice still shaky, snatching back her hand.

"It was one for this purpose," he said. He tried to push himself up to a sitting position, then winced and clapped his hand to his arm. "Ouch!"

"You're really hurt!" Nina said. Her mind was in a whirl. There was Charlie lying injured in front of her, but what happened to the bear? There was a bear, wasn't there? But then it wasn't. And then it was. She couldn't make sense of any of it, so she grasped onto the one thing she did understand. "Come on, we need to get you away from here! The bear..." She put her arm under Charlie's shoulder and helped him up.

He gave a little groan, then with his sound arm clasped Nina's, looking up into her eyes. "Nina, the bear is gone. You do not know *what* your kiss has done for me."

Nina caught her breath. Then, with an effort, she tried to turn his statement into a joke. "I told you it wasn't a kiss, I was just trying to do..."

"Please," he said, "let me thank you, my darling. You cannot imagine what you have saved me from." He was up on his knees now, as was Nina, facing him. He reached out his arm and drew her to him, holding her against his chest. "I can never thank you enough," he said, laying his cheek on Nina's hair.

Nina held still for a moment, breathing in his musky scent, letting her feelings wash over her. He was alive... "Oh Charlie..."

There was another loud cracking sound, and they jerked apart.

"What the—" Nina began. Had that been another shot? But it hadn't quite sounded right for a gun.

Charlie's head was raised; he was listening intently.

And there it was. "*Ah-wooooo-wow-wow-wow-awoooo!*" The high-pitched howl of a coyote, not very far away.

Charlie gave a groan. "The damn fool! I tried to keep him away from her house..." He rocked back onto his heels, then pushed up to a standing position, grasping his arm where the blood was starting to flow again.

Nina got to her feet. "What damn fool? What's going on?"

"It's a long story," Charlie said. "Damn, this really hurts!" He swayed on his feet.

Nina sprang to support him. "Let's get you inside!" she said, putting her arm around his waist. "And then we need an ambulance; you need to get this looked at!" She'd think about the coyote later.

"All right," Charlie said meekly, "let's go inside. I really can't stand up on my own two feet."

At his tone, Nina looked up suspiciously, and found that his eyes were twinkling down at her. Indignantly, she let go of him. "You're not nearly as bad as you're making out!" she said.

He grinned. "I won't say it doesn't hurt like hell," he said, "but no, I'm not at death's door. Although..." He raised his hand from his injury, and Nina saw that the whole sleeve of his jacket was saturated with blood.

"I know!" she said. "Come on then!"

His foot caught on a root, and he staggered. "Ow! I..." He flung out his good hand and caught himself against the trunk of the apple tree, leaving a bloody hand print on the bark. His head sank down on his forearm. "Hang on a minute, please," he said. "I'm kind of dizzy... The blood loss..."

Nina stepped back, took hold of his arm, pulled it around her shoulder and put her arm around his waist again. "You might be faking it, for all I care, but let's get you in the house so you stop bleeding all over my garden!" She guided him through the tangled bushes, found the patio steps and pushed him up them.

He gave a weak chuckle. "No, not faking it," he said as they approached the French doors. "Can't say I'm not enjoying your support, but not—oh!"

"Ow!" Nina cried at the same time. It felt like they had run against an airbag, a thick invisible barrier that kept them from going through the open French doors. "What the heck?" She reached out her hand, but met no resistance. "Come on—" She tried to push Charlie into the house, but there was that same feeling again, as if they had run into a rubber wall. "What's going on? Come on, let's go in."

Suddenly the barrier gave way, and they stumbled across the threshold. Nina just caught herself and Charlie before he crashed headlong into the mantelpiece.

"What the heck was that?" she said, trying to guide him to the couch.

He resisted. "I'd rather not bleed all over Miranda's cushions," he said. "Kitchen, perhaps?"

"All right," Nina said, "but don't weasel out of trying to answer. What *was* that thing? And why did it all of a sudden—I don't know—give way?" She took Charlie into the kitchen and deposited him in one of the chairs.

"It gave way because you invited me in," Charlie said. "It's a protection spell."

"It's a *what*?" Nina pulled the flannel jacket off Charlie's good arm.

"A protection spell. Miranda put it in pla—Ouch!"

Nina tried to ease the torn, blood-soaked sleeve of the jacket over the injury and winced at the sight of the mangled flesh. "This isn't coming off," she said, "I think we need to cut it."

"Scissors—in the drawer by the stove," Charlie said through gritted teeth, clutching his arm. "Damn, that hurts! I'd wish a curse on the guy who did this, if he hadn't already been caught in one."

Nina carefully sliced the fabric and gently peeled it away from the wound. "Why do I get the feeling that you're not talking metaphorically? Spells, curses—I'd say 'cut the crap and tell me what's really going on', but—after what happened out there..."

Charlie did not answer, and when Nina looked up, she saw that he had his head turned away and was clenching his teeth, trying to keep tears from spilling down his face.

"We have to call 9-1-1," she said. "You need an ambulance."

He shook his head. "No, no ambulance," he said. "Just try to do your best, it'll do."

"But I'm not a doctor or a nurse or anything! You need stitches in this! I'm going to call emergency. There's no cell reception in the house here, though, so I'll go outside and do it as soon as..."

"That's the protection spell," he said. "Nothing gets in that's not been specifically invited."

Nina raised her eyebrows. She took a dish towel, folded it into a thick pad, dampened it under the tap, then put it into Charlie's hand. "Here, hold that to it," she said. "We'll use a regular towel to keep it in place. I wish there was some way to stop the bleeding."

"Do you have any cayenne?"

"What?"

"Cayenne pepper. It can staunch blood flow."

"Really," Nina said skeptically.

"That's what I heard," he said. "Can't hurt to try."

"Uh, yeah, it can," Nina said. She rummaged in the cupboard. "But it's your funeral. Here, is this what we're looking for?"

She pulled out a small sealed can.

"If it says 'Cayenne', then yes."

"So what do you want me to do—dump it on?"

"Yes," he said, turning away his head again. "Try it."

Nina did what he asked. He hissed in his breath when the pepper first hit his wound, but then relaxed. "It actually doesn't hurt!" he said, surprised.

"If you were expecting it to hurt, why did you—hey, look, I think it's working!" The rapid flow of blood had slowed down, and it was forming dark clots. "That's—interesting. Okay, good, let's wrap it up until the ambulance gets here. Unless you would like some ketchup on it, as well, or perhaps a bit of sour cream." Nina collected a towel from the bathroom and secured the thick pad of cloth around Charlie's arm. "Hold that," she said. "Hang on, I think I saw some safety pins somewhere." She found them in the bathroom drawer, and once she had put them in place on the makeshift bandage, she scooped up the bloody and shredded flannel jacket and dumped it in the corner of the kitchen floor.

"Okay, ambulance," she said firmly.

"No, don't," Charlie said, catching her by the sleeve as she was trying to get past him to get to the living room. "I'm fine, honestly."

Nina pinched her mouth down. "No, you're not fine. But okay, I'll bite: why not an ambulance? Apart from the cost, of course." She pulled out the second kitchen chair, sat down, put her elbows on the table and her chin in her hands, and looked Charlie straight in the eye.

He looked down at the surface of the table. "I can't leave this property," he said. "At least not in this shape." He gestured down at himself.

"Uh-huh," Nina said. "That explains everything. *Not.* Come on, you have to do better than that."

Charlie gave a sigh. "It's a long story..."

"Well, if you don't want to go to the doctor, we have lots of time." Nina stood up and walked into the living room. "I even have snacks to keep us occupied during the telling." She came back into the kitchen with her cinnamon buns and the paper coffee cup. "It's cold now," she said, indicating the drink. "Actually, I guess we could warm it up on the stove." She pulled a small saucepan out of the cupboard and emptied the caramel macchiato into it, turning up the flame under it.

"Here you go," she said a few minutes later, putting a mug with half of the coffee in front of Charlie, "one caramel macchiato for here. And you're going to tell me this long story of yours." She slid the cold cinnamon bun out of its paper bag onto a plate, scooped the icing out of its plastic container, and put the plate next to Charlie's cup.

He inhaled the aroma of the coffee. "Wow, coffee... What kind did you say this is?"

"A caramel macchiato."

"I don't think I've ever had that before." He took a sip. "Mmm, delicious. And Cindy's Cinnamon Swirl Delight—she still makes those?"

"Yes. And you're stalling. Get on with telling me what you need to tell; I don't want to hear how long it's been since etc. etc."

"Actually, that *is* the story," he said, taking a bite of the cinnamon bun. "It's been—what is this, 2024? It's been twenty-eight years since I've had one of these... or a coffee..."

"Twenty-eight years? How old *are* you?"

"Thirty-one. Or I was, when I..."

"You mean you were drinking coffee at four years old?"

"No, obviously not. But my being four was a lot longer than twenty-eight years ago..."

"I don't get it."

"Well, that's because you're not letting me tell the story."

"Fine, then, I'll listen. Although it sounds very weird..."

"It is. But you'll have to suspend your disbelief. There are more things in heaven and earth, Virginia, than are dreamt of in your philosophies."

Nina bared her teeth at him. "Stop calling me that, and start telling. I won't interrupt then."

Charlie's Story

"I came from the UK in 1994," Charlie began.

Nina did some mental math. "So you were two? Did you come with your parents?"

"No. Stop interrupting." Charlie took another bite of his cinnamon bun. "Drink your fancy wossname coffee and just listen, will you."

"Okay, okay!" Nina took a sip from her coffee cup. "See, there! Drinking coffee, not interrupting."

"All right then. I came from the UK in 1994, *at thirty years of age*. There was a fellow I knew from uni who'd done treeplanting in northern BC, so I figured I would join him for a while. I did, and we made some good money. He decided to go back to the UK afterwards, get back together with his girlfriend or something, but I was bitten by the bug—I liked it here. So I stayed. Long story short, I ended up in Houghton, and I started picking up odd jobs here and there.

"It was only a week or two in that I met Miranda McManus at the Farmer's Market. I've always had a green thumb—get it from my Gran—"

Nina made a little noise in her throat.

"What?"

"Oh, nothing—just that my Granny loved gardens, too. More in the 'telling stories about them' way, but, still... And that's not interrupting, you asked!"

He flashed her a little smile. "So I did." He took another pull on his cooling coffee.

"So as I said, I have always had a green thumb and a liking for garden work, so I put it about that I was available. Miranda hired me on the spot, and I spent the next month digging and pruning and moving dirt and planting the seedlings she got in by mail order. I had a lot of fun, and Miranda—well, she became a friend, almost like a mother to me.

"But there were a few odd things about her. I didn't notice the protection spell she had on the house at first—it wasn't until much later that I ran into it, literally. She'd always made a point of inviting me in, stating the invitation out loud, so the spell was never triggered. But there was one day that I came when she wasn't expecting me. I made it into the garden, but as soon as I got to the porch I hit a wall. I was in a hurry and was going to take the porch steps at a jump, but I ran into the barrier so hard I was literally flung back onto my butt. I could not even touch the house. I made my way around the back side of the house, tried to knock on the patio door—but I couldn't make contact with the wall of the house. Well, you've seen it today. Unless I'm invited, I cannot come in."

"I thought you were being polite!" Nina said around a mouthful of cinnamon bun. She did not want to believe him—protection spells, too bizarre!—but she had seen it with her own eyes, felt it herself. "So why would Miranda lock you out of the house like that? I thought you were friends."

"Oh, it's not just me. It's everyone and everything."

"Oh! I saw one guy..."

"Exactly. It's not only humans, either. Haven't you wondered why the house is so clean and everything is in such good shape after so many years? Miranda didn't invite mice and woodworms into the place, so they couldn't come in."

"What about me? I didn't get an invitation."

"It's the invitation of the owner of the house that matters—and that's you now. You were invited by dint of inheriting the place."

"Hmm, I guess that makes sense..."

"Miranda was trying to keep herself safe, to protect herself," he continued. "And she used a spell to do it."

"That's... unusual."

"She wasn't the only person in town who had abilities like this. Miranda could cast spells, but she never used them selfishly, or to get advantages for herself. Those garden club ribbons she won she got fair and square, through hard work and green-thumbery.

"But there were others who were less scrupulous. One woman in particular—her name was—"

"Jadice," Nina interjected.

"Yes! How did you know?"

"I heard her name around. Heard stories about her. And saw her picture. I didn't like her from that, and I have a feeling I'm going to like her even less now."

"Jadice hadn't been in town all that long. Five or six years, maybe. Somehow, she heard about Miranda and got wind of what Miranda could do. I'm not sure how, because I don't think it was known in town—Miranda never talked about it—but maybe Jadice picked up on it because she had abilities herself. She'd bought the piece of property next to Miranda's, put a house on it, and—I don't know—maybe figured they would have a witches' coven or something out here, pool their resources, get their way in everything.

"But Miranda wasn't having any of it. She was a good enough neighbour, but what Jadice was proposing she didn't want to be any part of. So eventually she gave Jadice the cold shoulder, and boy, didn't that woman resent it! So that was the state of affairs when I came to town.

"Jadice was ... kind of sexy. Or at least she tried to be. She wasn't young anymore—somewhere around forty, if not more—but she had the works: plastic surgery, hairstylists, make up, anything that's humanly possible to give the appearance of youth. I am fairly certain she wanted Miranda's green thumb abilities to help her make it real in a magical way. But as I said, Miranda wasn't playing ball.

"So Jadice had to make do the old-fashioned way. And she did. There were plenty of fellows all over Houghton who fell for her and ready to make fools of themselves, but she wasn't interested in nice, mature—in other words, middle-aged—men. She was after young ones.

"There was one boy in particular that fell for her hook, line and sinker. He couldn't have been more than seventeen. Kind of a weedy, nerdy kid. He had it bad—he'd park his car by the road out here, and sit in it staring down her driveway... I think he fancied himself to be in disguise—he'd wear sunglasses and a baseball hat, and sort of slink down in his seat when he saw me coming. I didn't let him know I'd seen him, he was pathetic enough as is.

"Oh man, I still regret it..."

"What?"

"I put my foot in it. I told her he was out there, hankering after her."

"What? Why? And what did you have to do with her?"

He rubbed his hand down his face.

"I was doing some work for her by then—she'd hired me to deal with some of the landscaping outside that pink palace of hers. And I thought... I don't know what I thought. Like a damn idiot, I asked her if she knew about him sitting out there. I don't know what I was hoping to achieve, probably thought she'd let him down gently, politely tell him to leave. I hadn't quite got her number yet.

"She laughed—she had this particularly irritating laugh, like a girlish giggle gone rancid—and said 'No, really? A secret admirer! That I must see!'

"The next thing I knew, she was bringing the kid back down the driveway and into the house, and he looked like it was Christmas, his birthday and a big lottery win all rolled into one. I still can't believe I let her get away with that."

"Could you have stopped her?"

"No, probably not. I tried to say something to him a few days later when I was in town—his dad ran the tow truck business."

Nina made another noise, and Charlie looked at her with his eyebrows raised.

"Nothing," she said, "go on."

"He didn't want to hear anything I had to say about her. He was in love, and anyone who said anything against his inamorata was a skunk and a scumbag. Well, I tried... But after that, it was like Jadice was flaunting that kid in front of me. Every time I was at her place doing her shrubbery, there he would be—either showing up with a delivery of some errand he'd run for her, or just leaving, pretty much on the same pretext. Even in town she'd let him escort her around, to the point of letting him treat her to dinner at Margie's Diner. God, he looked so proud, and there she sat like some fat spider, with an indulgent look on her face that made it plain to everyone but him that she was just playing with him—and she would stroke his arm, and smile, and wiggle her cleavage at him..."

Ugh. And Nina had thought she was being too judgemental about that woman!

"It was sickening—and I must have let on that that's how I felt, because she thought she'd got what she wanted.

"Turned out that what she was really trying to do was make me jealous. She was using the kid to try to get to me, and she thought that my reaction was about that—that I was upset about her leading him on because I wanted her myself.

"So the next day, she was starting to put the moves on me. I'll spare you the gory details. She'd make me come into her house to change a lightbulb, or tighten a screw, and once she got me right into her bedroom. Actually, by that time she pretty much stopped pretending—she asked me to 'fix a broken lamp', which turned out to be nothing more than an unplugged power cord. I managed to extricate myself from that one, and when I came out, the kid was in the driveway. He must have seen me through the upstairs window, and he was devastated—you could see it on his face. Jadice, adding insult to injury, was calling after me, making it sound like something had actually happened between us. I tried to tell the kid nothing had, that I'd only come into the house for repairs, but he wouldn't hear me. He rushed off down the driveway, and I could hear him gunning his engine all the way down the road. I did tell Jadice off for that one, but she laughed and said he meant nothing to her. That was the bad part, I told her, and she should leave the poor kid alone.

"After that, I refused to go into the house. I still had her shrubberies to finish, and I wasn't going to break the contract, so I couldn't stay away from her property altogether; but I wouldn't go inside anymore. I tried to be polite about it at first, but she kept pushing. So finally I told her flat-out that I was not interested. Didn't want her, was not attracted to her, had no interest in sleeping with her, no thank you. I kid you not, that's how blunt I had to be. And even then she figured that if she could get at me physically, I'd change my mind—she literally threw herself at me, fell into my arms, tried to kiss me. I shoved her off, grabbed my tools and turned to leave.

"She was furious. It took her long enough to get it through her head that I was serious, but once it registered, she flipped out. I'd never seen anyone in such a vicious rage. 'I'll make you pay for this,' she said. 'Nobody turns me down. You are going to regret this.' She wasn't wrong, either... I have not regretted turning her down, but I bitterly regret ever laying eyes on that witch in the first place.

"And that's actually what she was—a witch.

"Just like Miranda was able to lay her protection spells around her house, Jadice put a spell around hers—a nasty one. And because I had turned her down by refusing to enter her house, and offended her by telling her off about the kid, it was exactly those two points she trapped me with.

"She knew Miranda's spell—I believe Miranda once shared it with her, early on before she knew what Jadice was. And she used exactly that spell, the 'you can't come in unless you are invited' one. But unlike Miranda's spell, which keeps people out without hurting them, Jadice's was actively malevolent.

"She liked to call men 'wild animals', she'd call me 'tiger' and 'bear'. That's probably where she got the idea for her curse.

"Did you ever read the Grimm's fairy tale 'Little Brother and Little Sister'? Where a brother and sister go into the woods, and there are enchanted rivers that say 'Whoever drinks from me will become a tiger,' 'Whoever drinks from me becomes a bear'? That's exactly what she did."

Nina shifted in her chair. "I read that story just the other day," she said. "Are you trying to tell me..."

Charlie nodded.

"She wove the curse into the protection spell. She must have called up the boy on the phone, and invited him into the house, timing it so he would get there right before me—she knew I was coming to clean up the last bit of the job. I saw her open the door to him and invite him in, then she left the door wide open so I could hear and see what went on. She was all over that kid. Even from a distance away I could see he was completely lost. I could not let that go, couldn't let her chew up that kid and spit him out.

"I gave a shout, but he was too far gone to hear me.

"'Go on upstairs, tiger,' she told him loud enough for me to hear, and gave him a shove in the direction of the staircase, 'I'll be right there!' He disappeared from my view, then Jadice turned around, looked me right in the eye, and pushed the door to.

"I saw red. She had gone too far. That kid wasn't a very prepossessing specimen, but he didn't deserve being used like that, I had to put a stop to it. I noticed that the door latch hadn't actually clicked shut, and I felt so clever for noticing it. I was going to go in, give her a piece of my mind, and get the kid out of there.

"I took two steps up onto her porch, and her curse hit me with a sound like a thunderclap. All of a sudden everything was different—the colours around me, the perspective from which I was seeing things, the scents that got into my nostrils.

"Then Jadice was there, laughing her repulsive laugh, and it sounded terrifying to my new ears.

"'Let that be a lesson to you, *my bear*,' she said, 'and see what woman will kiss you now!'

"I tried to stand up, to speak, but all that came out was a roar.

"She laughed again, and I tried to reach out, to grab hold of something to keep me up—but instead my clumsy paw went wide, and I hit her. Her mood changed in an instant, and she began shrieking at me.

"'You vile, miserable, foul beast, I'm going to kill you for how you have treated me!'

"And she shouted a spell and threw something at me. In my new form, I was terrified. I fell off the porch steps, taking half the porch furniture with me, turned, and ran. I literally ran for my life.

"'You are going to die!' Jadice shrieked after me. 'You—will—die!'"

"As I ran, I felt my throat closing up and a ringing in my ears; my vision went black.

"Instinctively, I had made for Miranda's house. There was a small gap in the hedge, and I pushed through it, the poison of Jadice's spell charring the hedge."

"Is that the same gap that's still there?" Nina asked.

"Yes," Charlie replied, "it never grew back." He shifted in the chair, then winced and clutched his arm.

"Are you uncomfortable sitting there? We can go in the living room."

Once they had made themselves comfortable on the couch, Nina said, "So you got through the hedge into Miranda's garden—then what?"

"Miranda had heard Jadice's shrieking. She was an exceptionally brave woman, and she didn't panic when she saw a frightened black bear crashing through her hedge. I don't know what made her put two and two together, but she figured out that it was me.

"'That witch! Now she's done it!' she said, and that was the last thing I knew until I woke up on the ground in her garden under the apple tree, feeling like myself again, except with a massive hangover. Miranda sat on the grass beside me, watching me.

"'I'm sorry, there is only so much I could do,' she said when she saw I was awake. 'I could only mitigate her curse in a small way. As long as you are in this garden, you will remain who you are. Outside of it, you are a bear.'"

Nina was gazing at Charlie, unable to take her eyes from his face.

"So you're saying that you... ??"

He nodded.

"I was the bear. For the last twenty-eight years, I've been a bear, anywhere but in this garden. Miranda was right, she had only been able to do a certain measure of things, and even those incompletely. She very much regretted it, and kept trying to find another solution, but none worked.

There was one way to break a curse like that, she said, after I told her what Jadice had done and said—Jadice had given me the clue. It was downright stereotypical..."

"A kiss?"

He nodded again.

"'Every curse can be broken,' Miranda said, 'you just have to know how.' But Jadice had also been right—she had tied me up in a tight knot. What woman would want to kiss a bear?

"However, what Miranda had been able to do for me was to give me a refuge, a place where I could be myself—even though it was only for a time. Jadice's curse had a hard grip on me—even in the garden here I was not safe. As it turned out, the curse wavered in its hold on me. Periodically, it would loosen its grip, and I was able to come into the garden. I would go as far as the property line, wish myself here as hard as I could—and there I would be. But after a time, the curse would snatch me out again, back into my bear form; there was nothing I could do to predict when or to stop it. And if I left the garden, as soon as I crossed the property line, I snapped into bear shape; I can't set foot beyond the hedge in my human shape."

"Ah, hence not wanting the ambulance?"

He shrugged.

Nina's head was in a whirl. How could she believe any of this? *Why* was she believing it? Because she was. She believed every word of what he had told her, incredible though it seemed. After all, she had seen him shift in front of her very eyes...

Suddenly she gave a gasp and clapped her hands to her mouth.

"The bear spray! Oh my God, that was *you*! That's why... Oh my God, oh my God, I am *so* sorry!"

He gave a little sideways smile and tipped his head.

"You weren't to know," he said. "How could you suspect that the bear wasn't just a bear?"

"Well, yes!" Nina said, getting indignant. "And the bear—or, well, you—scared the crap out of me! What did you do that for??"

"The first time you surprised me as much as I surprised you," he said. "In that moment, I forgot that I was in bear form, and I opened my mouth to say hello to you—but instead, I roared at you and frightened the hell out of you. Believe me, I was very sorry."

"Hmph, so was I! I don't think I've ever been that terrified in my life!"

"Well, when I thought about it, I realized that it was just as well I had scared you off Jadice's property. I was hoping it had been enough for you to never come back. And then when you drove up in the car the next day I tried to frighten you away deliberately, for my sins... Don't you see, darling—that witch's curse is still active, the same as Miranda's is still working after all these years."

Nina blinked. "Oh! Oh my gosh—you mean..."

"I'm fairly sure that every human who takes a step into that house will be turned into an animal. I'm very much afraid that's what happened to the hunter fellow who gave me this." He touched the towel bandage on his arm. "I tried to scare him off, but..."

"Oh my gosh! Poor Jerry!"

"Jerry? You mean..."

"Yes! It's Jerry who came after you with a gun, came after 'the bear'—he is that kid that you were talking about, isn't he?"

Charlie looked stunned. "Yes, the boy's name was Jerry! But..."

"Jerry's family runs the tow truck business. It's his brother now who drives the truck, and Jerry has a bookstore next to Cindy's café, but he's still mooning after Jadice. And—oh my God—" Nina dropped her head in her hands. "It's my fault," she mumbled, then she looked up at Charlie. "I'm so terribly sorry—it's my fault he came after you and shot you. *I* told him there was a bear by Jadice's house, and he kind of freaked out..."

"And that's why he came stalking me," Charlie said. "Oh God, the poor idiot. Well, I think we are even now, you and me—I scared the bejeezus out of you twice, and you pepper-sprayed me and got me shot..."

"Please," said Nina, her face in her hands again, "please don't mention it..."

Charlie laughed, an easy, free laugh that sounded as if he had not really laughed in years. Then he reached over, pulled Nina's hands down, and turned to look in her face.

"I lie," he said, his tone now serious. "We are not even. We can never be even. You have saved me—you have broken the curse. Without you—without your kiss ..."

Nina blushed a deep red.

"I told you," she said, "it wasn't a kiss! I was trying to do mouth-to-mouth resuscitation..."

"Hush," Charlie said. "It was a kiss, because it worked. You saved my life, you broke the curse. I am me again. But if you don't feel it was real—here." He took Nina's chin in his hand, tipped up her face, and lowered his head to hers.

Their lips met, and there was no doubt about it—that *was* a kiss. A fantastic one.

Free

Charlie smiled down at Nina.

"There! Was that a real kiss?"

Nina knew her cheeks were flushed, and she was breathing fast.

"Uh, yeah, I think so," she said, and she bumped his good arm with hers.

"Ow!" he said. "Easy there, I've just been shot!"

Nina suddenly sat up straight. "Wait a minute!" she said. "What makes you think the curse is broken?"

"I can feel it," he said. "I was dying. Her death curse took hold of me when Jerry shot me; it felt like when she first cast the curse. And then—I woke, and you were kissing me."

"Doing mouth-to-mouth." She smiled at him.

"Kissing," he said firmly, leaned over and demonstrated. "Every time you say it wasn't a kiss I shall have to give you another to teach you to call them by their proper name."

"Hmph! Full of yourself, aren't you?"

"I am—full of *myself* again, finally!"

"So, about that—you think you're you again because you *felt* it?"

"Yes."

"So what makes you think that you can't go outside the property?"

He did a double take. "Oh! I, uh... I suppose I got so used to thinking that..."

Nina bounced up from the couch and held out her hand to him. "Come on! Let's check!" She took a hold of his good hand and pulled him to his feet.

"So why," Nina asked as they were pushing their way through the front yard tangle, "didn't you just ask me for a kiss?"

"I tried to—well, to hint at it anyway. But it has to be freely, voluntarily given, not on request—Miranda and I talked about it long and in depth. If I had asked you to kiss me, or snatched a kiss myself, the best-case scenario would have been that it would not have worked—at worst it could have backfired."

"You mean it might have permanently beary-fied you?"

"Perhaps. I didn't want to risk that."

"Can't say I blame you."

"Or even worse, it might have turned you into a beast too."

Nina shuddered. "Oh my goodness, thank you!" She pulled open the garden gate in the hawthorn hedge. "All right, here we are. The wide world awaits." She flourished her arm at the street beyond the gate.

Charlie hung back with an uncomfortable look on his face.

"Aw, come on," Nina said, "don't be scared. If you turn into a bear again, I'll kiss you better, I promise. Deal?" She reached out and took his hand, ready to lead him out.

He hesitated.

"Fraidy-bear! Come on, you'll be all right." She tugged on his hand.

He took a deep breath to steel himself, but Nina wouldn't let him wait any longer. She dropped his hand, reached up with both hers, cupped his cheeks, and pressed her lips to his in a long, solid kiss. While they were lip-locked she stepped backwards, pulling him with her out through the gate.

He made a little "ouch" noise against her lips as the branches of the hawthorn snagged at his injured arm, but Nina kept kissing him and pulling him until they were three feet out into the street. Then she let go, stepped back and looked him up and down.

"There!" she said. "Now *that* was a kiss. And see, you're here. Out on the street, with two arms, two legs, and only a little bit of fur." She reached up and ruffled his hair.

Charlie drew in a deep breath and looked around in wonder. Then he reached out his good arm, pulled Nina close and buried his face in her hair. "I'm here," he said, his voice breaking, "I'm free..."

Nina wrapped her arms around him and hugged him hard.

"Now," she said when they finally let go of each other, "about that ambulance."

"I don't need one," he said, "I really don't."

"Okay, maybe not an ambulance, but a hospital. There's got to be one around."

"There wasn't twenty-eight years ago," Charlie said. "Just a doctor's office."

"Okay, that'll have to do then," said Nina. "I'm sure they can get you stitches. I'll drive you."

He sighed, but it was only half-hearted. "Very well then. I won't have health insurance anymore either, though; it could get expensive."

"Better than paying an *arm* and a leg, haha," Nina said. "Seriously, you need that stitched up so you don't lose it. I'm going to get my purse."

Charlie followed her back into the yard, but he stopped at the bottom of the porch steps.

"What?" Nina said, turning around at the front door. Then she remembered. "Oh. Sheesh, this is a pain. Why didn't you say something, ask me to invite you in?"

"Can't," he said. "Can't knock, can't verbally request admission. It has to be freely..."

"...freely extended, I bet," said Nina, rolling her eyes.

"Exactly so."

"Okay, fine!" Nina drew a deep breath. "I hereby invite you, Charlie—what was your last name again?"

"Hayward."

"All right, Charlie Hayward,"—Nina raised her voice, shouting her declaration into the trees—"you are hereby invited to enter this cottage whenever and through whichever door, window or,"—Nina looked around—"or chimney stack you please. This invitation is effective now, and valid forever. There, will that do?" she added in a normal voice.

Charlie got a wide grin on his face. "Whenever and however—forever? Do you really mean it?"

Nina shrugged, feeling a little self-conscious. "Well, I trust you not to abuse it. Did it work?"

Charlie lifted his foot and put it on the bottom step of the porch, then with a bound he got to the top of the stairs. "Yes! Yes, it did. Ow!" He clutched his arm and doubled over.

"Doctor's office," Nina said. "And stop jumping around like a jackrabbit, it's bad for your arm."

She got her purse, locked the door, and took Charlie back out to the car.

"That's the road down to Jadice's place, the back way," Nina said as they drove past the first turnoff on the left. "That's where I ended up going when I was trying to follow your directions that first time—you said to take the first left, and this is it."

"Oh!" Charlie said. "Good lord, I'm so sorry. This wasn't here when I was still driving those roads."

"Yes, figures," Nina said, shifting into third gear. "So, those last twenty-eight years—how have you been living? Like a regular bear? Were you conscious of your surroundings, I mean, like a human, or like a bear?"

"It's hard to describe," he said. "I think it was some of both. Well, of course I have no idea how a real bear experiences life, what he is aware of or not. For myself, I lived like a bear a lot of the times, but I kept going back to the garden, and when I was there I was fully human. I did watch other humans sometimes—there is a house where I could see the television through the window. It allowed me to keep track of what was going on in the world, the changes that took place."

"So you heard about 9-11, and all that?"

"Some, yes. And I know that there are new portable devices that were not in existence when I—well, transformed."

"So when exactly was that?"

"1996."

"Oh man, yeah. So many changes. I was only two... So how did you eat while you were out there?"

"Some of this and some of that. I'm afraid I did a bit of stealing here and there from humans—while I was a bear, of course."

"Oh! The wine and the loaf of bread?"

"Yes—sorry about that... The wine was a bit tricky to pick up; it's hard to handle things when you don't have opposable thumbs. The bread, I could stick my claws into."

"That's why there was that weird hole in the bread! So who did you swipe them from, do you remember?"

"If I think hard I probably can remember. It's a house over the ridge, this side of Houghton. I suppose we should replace the bottle of wine, at least, shouldn't we..."

"Yes. That was a nice wine; they'll have missed it."

"The other thing I did," Charlie said, "was eat the fruit and vegetables from the garden. I cleaned up the garden now and then—weeded and pruned, that sort of thing—but more often than not, when I came back it was all back to its overgrown state. There was still enough produce for me to enjoy, but I could not keep up with the maintenance."

"Hmm." Nina had her eye on the road. "So I wonder—was Miranda intending for this to happen? For me to, well, spring you free from the curse? Is this why she left my getting the property until now?"

"I believe so. She said she had a plan, and I would have to be patient. During the first year or two after I fell under the spell, she'd sometimes invite young ladies to her cottage, but I only met one or two of them, and only once each—my appearances were too erratic to set it up properly. Plus, there was never any real spark with any of them for me. Unlike..."

Nina darted a look at him out of the corner of her eye, and found him looking at her with an intense expression in his face. She willed the blush to recede from her cheeks.

"Why did Miranda leave it this long, I wonder? I could have been out here years ago, but I didn't even know she existed."

"She told me once that with spells of this kind, things often need to run their appointed course until the time is right."

"Kind of like Sleeping Beauty?"

"I suppose. Also—and mind you, this is just a guess, but having known her, it would fit. She and your grandmother were friends, and she was your godmother."

"She never did anything godmotherly, ever!"

"Exactly. I wonder if she was trying to make up for that, do you a good turn. I was stuck in my bear shape and didn't age in that time. I think she wanted *you* to be the one to break the curse, and so she waited with giving you the cottage and bringing you here until you caught up to me in age."

"Hmm. I guess that kind of makes sense... I wonder what happened to her though."

"I don't know for sure, but she'd sometimes talk about having a hankering to go see the Alps. I think she had a friend abroad somewhere—Switzerland, or Austria. "

"So you think she went to stay with her?"

"Him," Charlie said with a grin.

"Oh! Maybe that's the guy in the pictures in the album! Kind of blond moustache, 70's style. Looked rather smitten."

"Could well be," Charlie said. "And as she never came back, I think that's where she spent her last years."

"I wish I could have met her," Nina said as she geared down and made the last turn that took them into Houghton.

"Yes," Charlie said. "You would have liked each other. Oh, this place hasn't changed much, has it?" He was twisting his head around, looking at the town.

"That doesn't surprise me," Nina said, slowly driving up the main street towards the lake. "So, where would this doctor's office be?"

"That building is new," Charlie said, pointing at the hardware store next to the IGA. "And this one as well." There was a two-story square modern building with lots of glass that stood in one of the side streets, the sign in front of it declaring it to be "Houghton Professional Building." "Actually, that's where the doctor's office was back then," Charlie said. "In this old building, circa 1950s."

Nina pulled into the little parking lot beside the building. "Let's go see," she said, "maybe that's where it still is."

Her hunch proved correct. The medical clinic was on the bottom floor of the building behind one of the glass walls, with a comfortable-looking older lady behind the reception desk, her grey hair neatly set in a perm.

She looked up when they entered.

"Oh my goodness!" she said. "What have you done to yourself, young man?"

Charlie and Nina looked at each other.

"Accident," said Nina.

"With a shotgun," Charlie put in.

"He needs stitches."

"Well, yes, of course!" The receptionist bustled out from behind her desk. "Now you sit yourself down here, dear, and rest. Doctor Singh will be with you as soon as possible. Do you have his care card, dear?" She looked at Nina.

Nina gave her a blank look. Why would she have Charlie's care card?

Charlie chuckled. "She thinks you're my girlfriend," he explained. "Sorry, ma'am, I do not have a medical insurance card; I, uh, have only been here a short while." His British accent had suddenly become much more pronounced.

"Ah, yes," Nina stuttered, "we're, umm, staying in the same place, we're not together!"

"Not yet," Charlie said under his breath. The older lady gave him a maternal smile.

"So you're visitors then?"

"In a manner of speaking, yes," said Nina. "I'm from, uh, Vancouver, and Charlie is from—"

"Derbyshire," he said with a wan smile, clutching his injured arm. "Do you know how long the doctor will be?"

"Not long now," the receptionist said. "She should be done her last appointment any time. Can I give you a cup of coffee while you are waiting, dear? You look like you could use a stimulant."

"That would be lovely, thank you so much," Charlie said, still in that exaggerated accent and weak tone. Nina gave him a look. What a ham—his face looked perfectly normal-coloured, nothing like that horrible pallor it had before.

A few minutes later, a woman with a little boy came out of the consulting room, and the doctor, a sensible-looking woman in her forties, collected Charlie.

"Your friend looks familiar," the receptionist said to Nina. "There was a young fellow around here twenty-five years ago or so that he very much reminds me of—his name was Charles, as well. But of course he'd be much older now."

"Uh..." Think quick, Nina! "I—I think Charlie mentioned an uncle that he was named after."

"Ah, that could well be it! He seems like a nice fellow, your Charlie."

Nosey small-town people... But actually, Nina kind of liked it. And the lady was right, Charlie *was* a nice fellow. A very nice one, in fact.

"So will you be around here a while?" the receptionist asked. "It's a lovely time of year here, especially with the lake. You won't have that in the city, I wouldn't think."

"No, not where I live," Nina said. "I don't know how long I'll be staying... Actually—you wouldn't know of anyone who is trying to buy a house, would you? You see, I've inherited this cottage, and I can't afford to keep it, so..."

"Is that so? Right here, in Houghton?"

"A ways outside of it."

"Who did you inherit it from?" The receptionist shuffled the papers on her desk.

"Her name was Miranda, Miranda McManus."

The lady sat up straight. "Miranda! Well, of all the things—after all these years. How did you come by knowing Miranda—you're not a granddaughter, are you? I don't recall her having any children."

"I actually *didn't* know her," Nina said, wondering how much she should tell this nosey but knowledgeable lady. "It was my grandmother that did, apparently."

"Ah, I see! But I don't recall Miranda having a Chinese friend."

"My granny passed away quite some time ago," Nina said. "And she was Japanese, not Chinese."

"Oh, I'm sorry! I should know better by now. Dr. Singh is always calling me out for what she calls my 'white blinders'. It's a shame you're selling the house."

Nina nodded—she was beginning to think so herself.

"I can't afford to keep it. Especially now; I just lost my job."

"Oh, I am sorry to hear that," the lady said, and there was genuine sympathy in her voice. "There are not a lot of jobs to be had in a town like this. None that I can think of at the moment—unless you happen to be a legal secretary?"

Nina slopped coffee out of her paper cup.

"Come again?"

"George Harmon—he's our notary public—his secretary went on maternity leave and probably won't come back to work, and of course he can't get anyone else in a small place like this. He might have to shut down his office."

"But—but that's what I am! I'm a legal secretary!"

"Are you now! Well, well, well—isn't that a coincidence! Would you be interested at all then? It's not everyone's cup of tea to live in a small town like this, of course, but, dear, that would be wonderful! Ah, and there is your Charlie again. I'm sure you'll be feeling much better now, aren't you, dear?"

She started bustling around Charlie, who was being ushered out of the doctor's office, his arm neatly bandaged in white and secured in a sling.

"Do you want to keep the towels?" the doctor asked Nina briskly. "Charlie tells me they're yours. You did a good job with first aid there; it could have been a lot worse for him."

"Hah, he didn't even want to come in here for stitches!" Nina said. "I had to twist his arm to get him here—metaphorically, of course. And yes, please, I'd like the towels; I don't have a lot of them."

"Just think, Dr. Singh, this young lady has inherited Miranda McManus' house!"

"Has she?" the doctor said dryly. "Good for her. I don't believe I ever met Ms. McManus. Could you be so good as to get a bag for those towels, Noreen?" She turned to Charlie. "So keep that arm elevated, and if there is excessive swelling or pain by tonight, call or come back in. Don't make your friend drag you again, that's false heroism." She looked at Nina and gave her a quick smile. "His dressings should be changed every day. You can either bring him back here or do it yourself, if you feel comfortable with it. I've given him some sterile pads, and you can get more at the drugstore."

The receptionist came bustling out of the examination room with a white plastic bag holding Nina's blood-soaked towels.

"Here you are, dear," she said, handing it to Nina. "So how is your uncle these days then, Charlie?"

He gave the lady a blank look.

"Your *Uncle Charlie*," Nina said with a pointed look, "the one *you told me about*, that was working here for a while *back in the nineties*!"

His face cleared. "Oh! Yes, of course, good old Uncle Charlie. He's fine, quite fine! He has an, uh, garden centre back in Whitby, and he weighs at least twenty stone."

"Twenty stone? What's that in pounds?"

Charlie scratched his head. "Uh, somewhere around two hundred and eighty, I believe."

"Almost three hundred pounds? No!" Noreen said. "That's too bad—he used to be quite handsome."

"Ah, yes." Charlie grinned. "When he found out I was coming here, he asked to be remembered to, uh, the lady at the doctor's office—Noreen?"

"That's me!" the receptionist said, evidently pleased. "I wouldn't have expected him to remember!"

"Oh, he said he particularly remembered you," he said. "You were very kind to him when he had that strep throat in the winter of '95, he said."

Nina cleared her throat. "Charlie, we should go—you need to get some rest," she said.

"Oh, all right, darl—"

"Don't," she said with a warning glance at the receptionist.

The lady smiled at them. "Just like your uncle, he was such a flirt, too. You'll want to watch yourself around this one, dear," she said to Nina.

"Oh yes," Nina said, "I've figured that out already. Now, Charlie hasn't got insurance—how to we go about paying the bill?"

Ten minutes later they were sitting back in Nina's car in the parking lot.

"You didn't have to lay it on quite so thick about your Uncle Charlie," said Nina. "Three hundred pounds—sheesh. And him remembering that lady..."

Charlie laughed. "The last bit is true, actually—I do remember how nice she was when I had strep throat. There were a lot of nice people in this town. Quick thinking, by the way, about Uncle Charlie. I can keep using him. There might be more than Noreen who remember me."

"Are you planning to stay here then?" Nina shifted the car into reverse and backed out of the parking stall, giving Charlie a glance as she turned her head.

Charlie looked thoughtful. "I'd like to," he said.

"What would you live on?" Nina had paid the doctor's bill with her credit card, giving the excuse that Charlie had forgotten his wallet. It was three hundred dollars she couldn't really spare at the moment, but you had to do what you had to do.

She parked the car in front of the drugstore.

"I wonder..." he said. "I might actually still have some money available. I made some investments not long before—"

"Before Jadice happened?"

"Yes. And when—that—happened, and I was trapped in Miranda's garden, I gave her the ability to manage those funds. Signed some papers and what not. She sold my truck and my tools, and deposited the money in my investment accounts. Maybe that money is still there?"

"I don't see why not," Nina said. "And after twenty years, it might have accumulated a bit of income."

They got out of the car, went into the drugstore, and stocked up on first aid supplies to doctor Charlie's arm.

"I'll have to pay you back for all of that," Charlie said while Nina stowed the bag in the trunk of the car. "And the doctor's bill, too, of course."

"I'd say 'don't worry about it,'" Nina said, "but to be honest, I can't afford to. So if you can give me back at least some of it, that would be appreciated."

"So what about yourself?" Charlie said. "What are you planning on now?"

"Well, I *was* going to sell the cottage..."

"Was?" He was looking at her with a hopeful gleam in his eye.

"The receptionist lady—"

"Noreen."

"Yes, her. She said there might be a job for me here, with a local solicitor."

"Nina! That's fantastic!"

"I know, right? I got his contact info from her—that's what I was doing at the end there, while you were already in the car. It would only be a couple of days a week, but if I didn't have to pay rent..."

"Would you stay?" That hopeful gleam had become a beacon.

"I might." She put the key in the ignition, stepped on the clutch, and turned on the car. Then she turned it back off again.

"You know what?" she said, smiling at him. "I feel like celebrating. What would you say to another couple of cinnamon buns from Cindy? The coffee shop is right there."

"I'd say 'yes, please'!" he replied with a big return smile. "If—or let's say when—I get hold of my money, I'll take you out for a real meal, my treat. That's a promise."

When they walked into Koffee and Krumble, the cinnamon smell hit them right it in the face.

"Well, this place hasn't changed in twenty-odd years!" Charlie began loudly.

Nina bumped her elbow into his, clearing her throat.

"...according to what Uncle Charlie told me!" Charlie added hurriedly.

She grinned at him. "Good catch."

The teen barista recognized Nina.

"Oh, hi, you again?"

Nina blinked. That was right, she had been here earlier. Had it really been that same day? Only a few hours passed between the last time she had stood in the coffee shop, and now? Crazy thought.

"You're just in time, we're closing in five minutes," Caleigh said. "What can I get you guys?"

"Two caramel macchiatos, and a couple more cinnamon buns."

"Cindy's Cinnamon Swirl Delight," the barista and Charlie said at the same time.

Caleigh looked at him and laughed. "You've been here before!" Then she did a double-take, and looked from Charlie to the picture behind the counter. "Wait a minute—isn't that—" She pointed from the picture to

Charlie and back again, wrinkling her forehead. "Ah, no, doesn't work. Too long ago. Huh? What gives?"

Charlie grinned. "My uncle," he said easily. "He told me about the amazing baking here."

"Oh!" Caleigh's wrinkled forehead smoothed out. "That's why you were asking about the guy in the photo, right?" she said to Nina. "Because he looks exactly like him."

She started pulling the drinks. "I'm going to have to give you this stuff to go," she said, "because I have to close up. But if you want to eat it here before you go, you can take it into the bookstore and go out that way, Jerry is still there."

Nina's and Charlie's heads popped up, and they stared at each other.

"Did you say," Nina said carefully, "that Jerry is in the bookstore?"

"Yeah, he is," the girl said with a nod. "A good thing too; I was getting tired of babysitting the store. He came back around two-thirty. And you know what?" She leaned over the counter and lowered her voice. "He said thank you to me for watching his store, and apologized for being AWOL so much the last week. That's a new one, I tell ya!"

Nina and Charlie exchanged a glance. Had the gunman not been Jerry after all?

Caleigh put their drinks on the counter and the clamshell with the cinnamon buns next to them, and Nina handed her her credit card.

"Hey Jerry," the girl called out, "I'm gonna lock up. I gotta couple of customers with drinks here though, can they come through to the store?"

"Sure, send 'em on over! As long as they don't spill on the books!" The voice sounded like Jerry, but the tone of it was far more positive than Nina had heard before.

Charlie picked up the cinnamon bun container in his good hand and tipped his head in the direction of the bookstore, raising his eyebrows in a question. Nina nodded. She stowed her wallet and picked up the drinks.

"Thanks, Caleigh. See you again soon."

"No problem!" The teenager went over to the arched doorway between the coffee shop and the bookstore and started pulling a grate out of a pocket panel in the wall. Nina and Charlie stepped through, and she locked it behind them, turned around, and went back into the empty coffee shop.

Nina and Charlie looked around the crowded bookstore. The place behind the sales counter was empty—but then Jerry walked out from between the bookshelves, looking down at a book in his hands.

"Oh, hi," he said, "take your time with your drinks, I don't close 'til—" He looked up and stopped dead in his tracks. His mouth dropped open, and he looked back and forth between Nina and Charlie.

"Hi, Jerry," Nina said. "Remember me? I was in here a couple of days ago, asking some questions about some old pictures. And you gave me a jump start for my car."

He slowly put his book down on the counter.

"Yeah—yeah, I remember you. Extremely well, as a matter of fact. And you..." He looked at Charlie. "You look exactly like—but you can't be, can you?"

"My Uncle Charlie?" Charlie's voice sounded like he had a frog in his throat. "I've—ahem!—I've been hearing that a lot lately."

"I'll bet," Jerry said, running his palm over the top of his head. He put his hands flat on the counter and leaned on them, staring down at the surface, then he shook his head and looked back up at them. "Okay, this is the most bizarre coincidence—but I was just thinking about that guy—your uncle, did you say?—this afternoon. We have a bit of history from way back, more than twenty years ago."

"Oh yeah?" Charlie said casually. "Were you friends?"

Jerry scoffed. "No. Definitely not. I think he was trying to be nice, but..." He looked at Nina. "Do you remember my telling you about this—this woman that lived out in the woods, next door to Miranda McManus' place?"

Nina nodded.

"Well, you said there was a bear out there. I don't know what came over me, but I took my brother's gun out and went after it. And being back out there, man,"—he ran his hand over his hair again—"it brought it all back. It was like I was seventeen again—scary, I tell you. You know what you're like when you're a kid, eh..."

Nina exchanged a glance with Charlie. So it *had* been him.

"I felt exactly like I did in those days, except I didn't have a gun then. When that guy—your uncle, I guess—was hanging around, and it used to make me spittin' mad. Good thing I *didn't* have a gun then, I don't know what I would have done. But today I had one. And then that bear showed up. Except I didn't feel scared of it like I should have done, like it was a real bear, but I felt like it was that guy again, hanging around Jadice... So I pulled the trigger. And the bear roared at me, and I shot it again. I got it, too, and it ran off.

"So you don't have to worry anymore—I don't think it'll be back.

"But the really bizarre thing is what happened afterwards. I felt really proud, like I'd won a fight with someone I'd hated for most of my life.

"And I wanted to see Jadice's house again, like I wanted to tell her what I'd done, that I'd won the fight for her. I hadn't been there in, like, twenty years, not since she left. I used to think it was the most amazing place, beautiful and everything. So I went up to the porch, and as soon as I set foot on the bottom step, it was like I got hit over the head. This huge noise, like a shot; then I felt all weird—strange smells and sounds and stuff—and I think I said something like 'What the hell', but all that came out was a big howl.

"I fell backwards off the porch, and I must have hit my head, because I was out for a while.

"And when I woke up, I felt totally different.

"I sat up and looked around, and I was still in front of Jadice's place, but it had changed. Or, probably, the way I saw it had changed. It looked shabby, and kind of tacky. I went back up on the porch and looked in the window, and everything in there is falling to pieces. Old paper and stuff on the floor, wallpaper peeling, all of that. And all of a sudden I thought that it was kind of like Jadice herself—great-looking at first glance, but close up you could see the paint peeling. It was all a sham.

"I don't know what I saw in that woman—I guess I was a kid, and you're kind of stupid at that age. And she was definitely leading me on, God knows why. Which is what you, I mean, your uncle—God, you look like him!—was trying to tell me back then. I just couldn't hear it, I was so under Jadice's spell.

"But it's over now. It's like somebody snapped on the light, and for the first time in twenty years I'm able to see."

He shook his head again.

"And I have no idea why I'm telling you all that... You must think I'm nuts."

"No, not at all!" and "Don't worry about it!" Charlie and Nina said at the same time, and then they all three looked at each other, and nobody said anything for a while.

Jerry finally broke the silence.

"Well," he said. He picked up three paperbacks, tapped them on the counter to straighten them, then laid them along the corner, precisely lined up with the edge. "So, you guys gonna stay around here for a while?"

"We might," Nina said with a smile, "we just might." She turned to Charlie. "Let's go, okay?"

He nodded, and they turned to the door.

"Hey,"—Jerry cleared his throat—"if you see your uncle—let him know that Jerry from Houghton says hi, eh?"

Charlie turned around, and the smile he gave Jerry was brilliant.

"I'll do that," he said, "you can bet on it."

Garden of Good Things

It was getting dark by the time they got back to the cottage. Nina parked the car, turned off the engine, and looked at Charlie.

"Well, here we are. Home again, home again, jiggety jig," she said with a smile. She reached for the shopping bag in the back seat. "Let's not forget our loaf of bread and jug of wine."

"... and thou, that's the most important part," Charlie said with an answering smile that sent goosebumps down Nina's spine.

She got out of the car and went around to the other side to help him manoeuvre out of his seat with only one hand, then she leaned back against the car and tipped back her head.

"Look," she said, "the stars are coming out!"

He leaned against the car beside her and looked up. "Yes, there's Polaris!" He pointed.

"Which one?"

He reached with his good arm around her shoulder so she could follow his pointing better.

"There, right up from the Big Dipper—see it, darling?" His arm casually settled around her shoulder.

"Don't call me dar—" Nina began, then she changed her mind. "Ah, whatever," she said and snuggled into his arm. "You can call me what you like, snookums."

He laughed out loud. "Snookums? All right, you win." He gave her shoulders a squeeze, then let go. "Let's go in, darling, I'm getting cold."

"Yes, let's," Nina said, pushing herself away from the car. She gathered the shopping bags into one hand, then gave her cell phone a couple of shakes to turn on the flashlight.

They carefully made their way through the tangle of grass and bushes by its light.

"The first thing we'll have to do is trim back this stuff," Nina said, pausing at the bottom of the porch steps. "Actually, no, the second; the first is to get you some new socks. Or, no, the third—we have to get the power connected. And see if we can get internet out here."

She noticed that Charlie was standing in front of the entrance door as if something was keeping him from going in.

"What? Oh no! Don't tell me my blanket invitation didn't work after all! Is the spell still keeping you out??"

He gave her a tender smile.

"No, darling, not the spell. Look, I got up onto the porch, all on my own."

"Then what?"

"The door is locked."

Nina groaned. "D'uh... All right, fine—the *first* first thing we're going to do tomorrow is get a key cut for you!"

"A key—for me?"

"Yes. I'm tired of having to issue invitations or unlocking doors for you if I want you in my house. And as I need you to help me get my garden in shape, you are going to be here *a lot*—in fact, you're going to be living here. So you need a key."

She pulled the key out of her pocket and unlocked the door.

"There you are," she said, pushing it open. "Go on in, you don't need an invitation anymore."

"Nina..."

She bumped him with the shopping bag, and he took the hint and stepped into the house. She followed him in, put her shopping bags on the floor in the hallway, then turned around to close the door, but Charlie's arm was there ahead of her.

He pushed the door shut and trapped her against it.

"You want me to come live with you here?" he said.

"Yes," Nina said, her heart beating in her throat. "I inherited a garden, and you were in it. You belong here—so you have to stay around, in my Garden of Good Things."

"Nina," he said, and in the darkness she could feel more than see that he was looking down into her eyes, "Virginia Marie Takahashi, my darling, I love you."

"Don't call me—"

But he stopped her with a kiss, and Nina didn't mind at all. She wasn't going to finish that sentence anyway.

"...and the little girl married the enchanted squirrel, and..."

"Granny?"

"Yes, sweetie?"

"I think I'd rather have a bear than a squirrel."

"Wouldn't you be frightened of a bear?"

"I don't think so. He'd roar at me, and I'd say 'be quiet' and bop him on the nose. And then he'd go make me a cup of tea."

"Very well then. The little girl—"

"She's a princess."

"All right. The little princess married the bear, and they lived happily ever after together in their Garden of Good Things."

About the Author

Angelika M. Offenwanger lives in rural Western Canada with her family, two cats, and a bear – but only a small stuffed one by the name of Steve. She wishes she were a better gardener, but lacking green thumbs, she creates gardens on the page. Online she can be found on Facebook and Instagram @amoffenwanger, and on her website at www.amoffenwanger.com.

www.ingramcontent.com/pod-product-compliance
Lightning Source LLC
LaVergne TN
LVHW091138080826
845145LV00008B/2188

* 9 7 8 1 9 8 8 2 7 3 1 6 7 *